GW00726872

Woman on the Edge of Reality

Linda Parkinson-Hardman

Crystal Clear Books
Dorset

First edition published by: Crystal Clear Books

ISBN: 978-0-9556906-3-1

A catalogue record for this book is available from The British Library.

Telephone: 0843 289 2142

Website: www.crystalclearbooks.co.uk

The book is dedicated to my Mum, Pat and my sister Beth who have always believed in me and to Stevie for having the foresight and love to pack me off to Cornwall.

Chapter 1
Friday

Rosemary stopped the car, unsure of where to go next. The directions had been clear, left at the T-Junction, right at the low bridge and then right again. The cottage was supposed to be next to the big house, but the one she was looking at looked nothing like the photo she had printed off the website the day before. An elderly man was close by and she turned in her seat to open the window to ask if he knew the cottage she was seeking, but he resolutely avoided catching her eye and not being sure of herself, let alone her bearings, she dug out the printed sheet and looked once again at the photo of the cottage and back at the one that was facing her. It was definitely not the right place; the door was on the wrong side to start with.

Sighing, she thought that she would carry on up the little lane to see whether that might be more fruitful. No sooner had she started the car and carried on past the house that sat to the front of the row of cottages than she saw it. Smiling to herself ruefully, she realised she'd done what she always did. Except on this occasion she wasn't wrong, she'd got it right and first time too. Perhaps this was going to be easier than she thought.

Trewelyan Cottage was an old miner's cottage, or so the website said. There had been little more than that, except that it looked pretty and inviting. She sat in the car and looked at her surroundings in more detail. It was in the middle of a row of twelve cottages, each one set back behind a large detached stone house, the mine managers' houses' perhaps, she thought. Each one had a long garden at the front with a small parking area.

The house to the right of hers was obviously occupied by a family, given the number of toys and play equipment that littered its front. She wasn't wrong as at that moment, she heard the shriek of a child whose toy had been taken away, followed by a long wail of frustration and anger.

Bugger, she thought, this was meant to be peaceful. The last thing she needed was to suffer the noise of small children crying and parents ranting.

She carried on looking. The cottage was stone, local granite she assumed, but her knowledge of geology was poor, so she couldn't be sure. Grey though and weathered, but not crumbling. It had three windows to the front, with two upstairs. The garden was slightly raised from the road and she couldn't see it clearly enough to make an assessment of it, but she caught the faint scent of rosemary on the wind, rosemary for remembrance!

Almost immediately she felt like crying, and reached for the box of tissues that had accompanied her on the long car drive. She looked at the mass of used ones in the foot well and resolved to clean the car out while she was in Cornwall, so that at least she'd be able to go home with a tidy car, if not a tidy mind.

She was suddenly aware of being watched and saw a small child staring at her from the garden next door, obviously the one that had objected strongly and vocally. She realised that it might look odd to be sitting in a car without doing anything, so she got out and stretched tired arms and legs.

The child moved and rushed back to the house, just as a young woman appeared with a baby in her arms. It was difficult to tell whether the child was boy or girl, all clothes looked androgynous these days and its hair was short. She guessed she'd find out if she were supposed to. The young woman smiled and raised an arm in greeting and the baby turned its head to see what its mother was looking at.

Suddenly she was embarrassed, three pairs of eyes were watching her and she was self conscious. She half waved back and turned to the car, deliberately letting the others know that the show was over. Reaching into the back seat, she pulled out her pillow, and one of the food bags she'd brought with her, hoicking her handbag onto her shoulder, she made her way through the front gate, and into the garden beyond. By the time she looked again, all three had disappeared.

The garden was delightful, if a little small. There was a bench underneath the window that was out of sight of the house next door and promised the luxury of being able to drink tea outdoors, something she couldn't do in her small apartment at home.

Dumping her belongings onto the bench, she cast about for the yellow upturned plant pot, which her host had promised hid the key to the house. She spotted it, reasonably well hidden under the rosemary bush she had smelt earlier and as she brushed the stems aside to reach under the pot, she released another rush of herbal scent. Breathing it in deeply, the tears threatened to start again. She crouched for a moment, composing herself before straightening up and moving back to the front door.

Once again, she gathered up the possessions she had brought from the car, awkwardly shifting the pillow from one arm to the other as she sought a way to easily get the key in the lock to turn it. Giving up, she put the bag of shopping down on the floor and that was when she noticed the leaflet that had been half pushed into the letterbox. Pulling it out from the wrong side caused it to rip, but she was curious. This was a holiday let, why would the postman put junk mail through the door. Opening it up, she saw it was an advertisement for the farmers' market, to be held the first Saturday in every month. It was Friday, tomorrow was the 4th and she resolved to walk down to the village in the morning.

She tried the key again and this time it turned easily in the lock, picking up the groceries, she made her way in to the tiny vestibule, paying attention to everything as she went. Coat hooks on the right, door mat before the inner door, boot hook on the floor; it all went in to her brain, even though she wasn't aware of what she was doing.

Opening the inner door she found herself in a small light room, dominated by an enormous stone fireplace that was constructed as a dolmen might be from two huge vertical pieces with another massive one acting as mantle. The fireplace housed a stove and she was pleased to see that there was a huge basket of fresh logs and that the stove was already stacked ready for lighting.

In front of the fireplace was a squashy sofa full of inviting cushions and covered with a throw, a rug completed the fireside ensemble. There was a TV, a dresser with a mirror above, a small bookcase and a dining table and four chairs. At the back of the room was an open tread pine staircase which looked freshly varnished and through an arch next to the fireplace was a tiny, newly fitted kitchen. Leaving her pillow and handbag on the sofa, she walked into the kitchen and left the bag of groceries on the worktop.

Resolutely ignoring the call of the kettle, she left the cottage and headed back to the car for the rest of her possessions. Her suitcase she took straight upstairs, her laptop she left near the dining table, the box of books found a home underneath the staircase and the remaining foods were taken into the kitchen. Ten minutes later the car was locked, the front door was closed and she had drawn fresh water for tea.

She stood for a moment in the kitchen and surveyed her surroundings. Cheerful, red check curtains hung from the window and outside all she could see was a dry stone wall with tufts of grass gamely hanging on in the crevices. Clearly the land at the back was higher than at the front, although it was still so light and bright she was confused for a moment or two, until she realised that there was a small pathway running along between the base of the wall and cottage, just wide enough to allow the light down. Perhaps she could explore that soon.

Quickly she put all her foods away; she'd brought enough for the whole week and felt a tinge of guilt at not supporting the local economy by buying at the village shop, and then dismissed it for the transient sense of responsibility that it was.

Instinctively she put everything in the place that most closely resembled home, tea bags, camomile tea and honey above the kettle, nuts in the jar to the left of the hob, cereals, tins and other dry goods in the cupboard that was empty; this last was confusing, the only place that wasn't the same as home and she wondered briefly whether she might move the contents out of the corner cupboard so that she could have something as familiar as possible.

The very act of catching that thought though ensured she wouldn't, that's just too sad and besides I'm here for a change, not for the same old, same old she thought. The tea cupboard would have to suffice as her taste of home.

It was as she walked back through the sitting room, preparing to go upstairs that she noticed that a place had been set for tea on the table. Six scones neatly arranged on a china plate with a matching teacup. A dish of jam was to one side and an enormous bowl of thick clotted cream beckoned to her.

Oh dear, that's not good she mused.

Part of her plan had been too do a detox of sorts and was the main reason for bringing everything with her as that way she could control more easily what she was eating.

But surely just one can't hurt? I'll come back to that later she thought and climbed the stairs to sort out her clothes.

She had brought little with her as her intention was to spend time alone, working, reading and walking. She hadn't come for fancy nights out and wasn't planning on talking to anyone either, so simple jeans, tee-shirts, leggings and some of her favourite knitted dresses were going to be the order of the day. She smiled to herself as she removed her favourite pink pyjamas and her hot water bottle too – she wasn't planning on not indulging herself though either.

There were two bedrooms, the one at the front of the house, the one with the double bed and the sky blue bedding was to be hers. It faced west and looked out over the fields towards the sea, if she looked hard enough she could see a thin ribbon of blue on the horizon. She guessed it was perhaps only a mile or so down to the coast path and from there she should be able to get down on to the beach. Optimistically, she'd brought swimming gear and a beach towel or two as well; you never knew what the weather was going to be like in England in September and the coastal waters were at their warmest at that time of year too.

Her wash bag went into the tiny shower room and it took no more than a minute or two to add her shower gel, shampoo and conditioner to the shower tray, her toothbrush and paste to the glass provided by the sink and her moisturiser to the shelf above the loo. She liked things neat and tidy, to feel at home wherever she was and it was her custom to always settle in by unpacking and lay out her things to mark her territory before she did anything else at all. She reflected as she worked that it always seemed to take longer to pack up to leave than it did to unpack for staying, but then she pushed the thought aside as she didn't need to worry about that until the following Thursday.

She opened the door to the second bedroom to peer in. It was half the size of the main bedroom and barely fitted the bed and the large chest of drawers. The single bed was un-made, but that had been fine, she had been quite clear when booking, she was coming alone, to be alone.

The view from the window was breathtaking. Moorland stretched out before her. The land was just at the height of the first floor now and she could see stones, mounds and the remains of tin mines, their tall chimneys visible on the skyline. It was as bleak as any inner city urban landscape with the rotting hulks of a once proud industry standing to lonely attention.

Sadness came upon her quickly, thoughts of the change that had been wrought over the years crowded into her head, people long lost, skills no longer practiced.

We had been a nation of builders once but what were we now she thought.

Turning away from the window she looked quickly behind the curtains that hid the room's storage area and found blankets, extra duvets and bedding. She grabbed a blanket, knowing of old that wrapping a blanket around her was the fastest way she had to feel safe and secure.

Making her way downstairs she looked more closely at the table. Underneath the china and afternoon tea was a red gingham table cloth and on the side plate were perfectly positioned a matching

9

cotton napkin and a knife just waiting for the moment it would spread the rich black jam and heaving cream across a silent, but compliant, scone.

She made a pot of tea, rare for her as she normally just threw a tea bag in the cup. Taking the teapot to the table she sat down and spread the napkin across her legs, chose a scone, not too big, but not too small either and home made by their shape. She cut it in half with a knife, remembering as she did so that good scones could simply be pulled in half. Cream on first, a thick layer that didn't move or run from where she placed it, then jam on top. It looked like blackberry but she wouldn't know until she tasted it. She poured a cup of tea and added milk from the jug and took a long gulp. Breathing in deeply for the first time in weeks Rosemary felt herself starting to relax.

The mouthful of scone confirmed her worst fears, she would have to put them away or throw them away because their deliciousness would overcome her poor discipline where food was concerned. Just one to eat now and the rest, she decided, would freeze and be taken home for later.

The jam was blackberry, with a hint of apple. Its scent hinted at long summer days ripening on the hedge, of early summer mornings in an orchard and she visualised for a moment, the place that these had been picked. It was clearly homemade; it was viscous and smooth and was unlike anything she had bought from the supermarket in recent years. It reminded her of her grandmother, whose house had been full of the scent of jams, chutneys and wines and whose bosom was where she had returned when some new or imagined hurt had happened upon her as a child.

Briefly, she wondered whether the child next door had a grandmother within walking distance that she could escape to as well.

The cream was the consistency of butter and reminded her of the days when she would fight her father to get the top of the milk on their cereals in the mornings, that was if the birds hadn't already beaten them both, pecking through the silver foil caps on the bottles outside the front door.

She savoured the moment, knowing that this time her resolve would last. She also knew that she had a treat in store when she returned home as the scones would go with her, so there was no sense of loss, simply an enjoyment of the moment, a decadence that would last the whole seven days through.

All too quickly the scone was finished and she was pouring a second cup of tea. She sat nursing it in both hands, wondering what she should do next. Immediately she was assailed by thoughts of duty, responsibility, by the huge folders of work she had brought with her to do, her excuse if you like for taking precious time out of her busy work schedule. Then a wilder, more rebellious thought kicked in. I don't need an excuse to be here, I don't need to do this work and in fact I don't need to do anything. If I wanted, I could just sleep the whole week away.

Glancing at her wrist she remembered she'd forgotten her watch and she couldn't recall seeing a clock anywhere in the cottage. Maybe that wasn't such a bad thing. She was driven by time at home; not enough to do this, not enough to do that and certainly not enough to be frivolous with. Yet, here she was taking time off with a flimsy reason that she would be able to catch up on all the things she never had the time to do at the office. There was no internet access, there was no phone ... phone, too late she realised her mobile phone was around somewhere.

It needed charging and yes, there was a clock on it, so she wasn't entirely without the means to manage time after all, but at least it wasn't sitting staring her in the face all day, she would have to make an effort to find out what the time was instead. In fact, if she wanted she could turn the phone off, forget what day it was and just let her body be ruled by the movement of the sun, moon and stars through the sky.

She decided instead, to plug the phone in and turn it on. She also set up a space to work at one end of the dining table. She found a socket and plugged in the extension cable she'd brought with her 'just in case' and set up her netbook, mouse and mouse mat. She put the pile of books she'd brought with her onto the book case and placed her pencil case, note pad and diary neatly at the head of her new desk. She had left herself enough space to eat and a placemat would ensure that remained the same throughout the week. She was a woman that liked routine, she liked to know what was going to happen next and invariably this meant she read the end of the book before she started, just so she knew she wasn't going to be disappointed. Sometimes this meant that she then missed out on the story too because it didn't seem worth reading it after all once she knew how it was going to end, but this wasn't something that bothered her normally.

Carefully, she returned the plate of scones to the kitchen and found a food bag to put the five remaining delicacies in. The whole lot were then deposited into the freezer where she knew she wouldn't have the heart to bring them out until she returned home. She was an instant gratification person, if she couldn't eat it there and then, the moment would be gone and she'd be able to do without.

In the sitting room, she poured a third cup of tea and sat down, by her laptop, with every intention of turning it on to read the first draft reports she'd brought with her. But the moment was lost, she hadn't acted quickly enough and instead she reached for her phone.

She pressed the button that sparked it to life, swiped a finger across to access it and was oddly disappointed that there had been no activity. No messages, no missed calls. It seemed, she thought, like she'd been forgotten already. Although she hadn't wanted any outside contact, not getting any was a different thing altogether. She put the phone down, resolving to try and avoid looking at it for fear of being disappointed all over again and picked up her cup of tea and took it to the sofa.

She sat, savouring the firm cushions beneath and behind her, thinking how nice it would be to light the fire and watch the flames, then realising again that it was early September and would probably make the cottage too hot.

As she sat, the silence surrounded her, except it wasn't silent. Simon and Garfunkel's song, 'The Sound of Silence' came into her head and for the first time ever she thought she had a glimpse of what they were referring too. She listened to the silence and became aware of her own inner sounds, a gentle buzz, against a background of clicks and whirrs which obviously meant her brain and body were in fully working order. She listened intently to the soft tick, tick, tick of her pulse in her ear and the gentle rumble from her belly.

She drank her tea and listened, aware of a tension draining out of her.

Her shoulders started to shrink back from around her ears, her legs felt heavy and her eyelids were on the point of closing. She fought the sleep that was overcoming her, but felt instinctively that she would rest well that night.

The experience was so gentle that she barely noticed the passage of the sun. She sat for what might have been hours, just becoming used to being.

Every so often her gaze would wander round the room she had found herself in, observing the stones in the fireplace; noting but not analysing their irregular size and placement, marvelling at the skill that had placed them 'just so', measuring by eye it seemed, rather than by yardstick.

As she looked she spotted more things to delight her senses. What had seemed simple suddenly wasn't; there were fresh flowers, red gerberas to match the curtain colours and a handful of sweet peas that were contributing to the fragrance of the cottage. Bundles of kindling lay next to the stove together with a bucket of coal and thick gloves for carrying things too hot to handle.

She wondered at the holes in the great sheaf of granite that was the mantle shelf, neatly drilled but containing nothing now. She had visions of spit roasts and dogs running in rings, but realised she was probably several centuries too late for that.

She spied old hooks and nails in the walls that had been covered over with fresh paint, wondering what had hung on them over the years. The carpet was new too and the whole cottage had an air of being well loved by its myriad of owners. This was no haunted place of sadness as it held a lighter feeling, one of joy and happiness and as she sat she allowed it to seep into her bones, into her very soul.

A dog barked in the distance and she started, bringing herself abruptly back into the present. Her tea cup was long empty and the light had started to lower and she felt the need to overcome the long drive with a walk to stretch leg muscles out of the unfamiliar shape they had seemed to adopt.

Grabbing her cardigan, slung casually over a chair, she put on light summer shoes and headed out the door, scooping the key off the dining table as she went.

It wouldn't do to get locked out she thought.

She walked past the car and turned right, back the way she had come when she had driven in and headed to the main road. Although there was no path to speak of, there was a deep verge and the road was quiet. All she had to do was move to one side should a car come alongside or need to pass.

She had no idea where she was heading, except for a vague notion that it might be nice to see where the beach was. She walked quickly up to a crossroads, encountering no one else along the way, neither car, nor cyclist nor walker, then turned right into the lane where the signpost pointed to a lighthouse.

As she walked she became aware of a dull ache in her left leg, but ignored it and simply walked faster to try to work the stiffness and discomfort of driving a long distance out of her body. She could spy the sea and the tip of the top of the lighthouse in the distance and was aware of heading slightly downhill.

The lane became more Cornish with every step she took and soon she was following a narrow road that was bordered by high hedges atop well concealed stone walls, there would be nowhere to go should a car decide to come too close, but she decided to ignore that problem determining to deal with it only should the need arise.

Round the next corner she was presented with a fork in the road, the right hand turn looked less well used than the lane she was on and was therefore more inviting to this new, adventurous woman that was emerging from within. She took it, and as she walked she became aware of vast numbers of blackberries hanging from the brambles on either side of the road. What a pity she'd not brought a bag with her, but no doubt they would still be here if she decided to walk that way the following day.

The fields on either side of the road were rock strewn and grassy; in some, cows grazed content to ignore one lone woman walking near them. She stopped once to look back the way she had come and was surprised to see how far away the cottage she was staying in was, she'd come a long way without realising it. The silence on her road was even louder than in the cottage. Birds were calling to each other, but she didn't know what they were. Cows occasionally mooed a response to some unknown question and all around her was the sound of the wind in the grass and the hedgerow. She was glad of her cardigan because the breeze was cool and the sun was sinking slowly in the west, the last of that day's warmth being given out and shared amongst the people of the land.

The smells were stronger too, that slightly autumnal tang, tinged with slurry and grass that is common in the country, but this also had a sharper note, a promise of salty sea and seaweed. It drew her on, eager to see the edge of the world as she thought of this part of her country. Beyond that shore lay nothing but the Atlantic and it was thousands of miles to the next direct landfall in America, in many ways the vastness of it was frightening; but it was exhilarating too.

She had come to the very furthest part of Cornwall, she was mired deep in the country where no one could find her and no one could contact her and if she decided to she could turn her phone off. She had told no one where she was going, simply that she was taking the week off, and here she was at a point where she could literally go no further without having jumped on a plane.

The road ended abruptly in a farmyard. The costal path and she assumed the way to the beach, was off to her right though the route was obviously little used because it was so overgrown. She stepped off the tarmac and onto soft earth that was still slightly damp from the heavy rain of the previous week. Cautiously she made her way carefully along the path; although it was mostly compressed mud there were slippery stones at irregular intervals and the land was dipping down even more steeply. There were nettles in abundance, a sign of the health of the land around, but not conducive to bare legs. Reluctantly she decided to abandon the walk in that direction until she was wearing something more sensible on her feet and her legs.

Turning back on herself she made slightly slower progress back the way she had come, she was tired and was now walking up hill, it no longer seemed so easy. But she was reluctant to change her plan and return to the cottage immediately, she still wanted her legs to feel well used and stretched and so when she returned to the fork in the road instead of heading back to the main road and the village, she turned right again and headed once more towards the lighthouse.

This road too was lined with brambles, laden with the fruit of early autumn and she was even more determined to return the following day with plastic bags for the picking of such a delicious treat as this. It would be completely in keeping with her planned detox and she could eat them, slightly cooked with the apples and honey she'd brought too. The thought pleased her and she realised that her spirits had lifted enormously since the start of the day. Slowly she reflected on why this might be the case and it came to her unbidden, that here she was just herself, she had no one to answer to and no one to 'be' either, that thought was intoxicating and her speed picked up again as she realised the sense of freedom she had just had a glimpse of.

There were people ahead of her now on the road; a couple, she somewhat taller than him both with cameras, tourists just like she was, strangers passing through for a brief moment in time. They stopped every now and then to admire the view, exchanging a brief sentence or two and to take a picture, images that would probably never see the light of day once clicked.

She wondered if they were staying in the village, perhaps at the guest house or the pub, perhaps they too had taken a cottage just as she had done. She started to construct a story around them, creating a perfect tableau to set them against before catching herself and recognising the habit she had of projecting out onto those people around her. Realising this, she also noted that the walk was going to be much further than she had anticipated; sure the coast was no more than a mile at most as the crow flies, but this lane wound backwards and forwards like a snake gliding across the sand. She was tired and she needed to eat so it was time to head back before the sun sank too far down beyond the horizon and it became to cold to enjoy the walk. Her fingers and hands were getting a little too cool for comfort and the pleasure of pink pyjamas and a hot water bottle were tantalising in the extreme.

She turned back up the lane and began the trudge back to the cottage. She hadn't anticipated how far downhill she had walked and it was an effort to expend the energy needed to propel her body along. As she walked, she thought and as she thought, she began to plan. Tentatively at first because it had been a long time since she'd had the luxury of planning on a holiday such as this for herself but by the time she had reached the main road again she had a half formed idea about how the rest of her week would look.

Reaching the cottage once more, she sat on the bench in the garden to see the last of the sun slowly wend its way to the other side of the world before letting herself in and locking the door behind her.

She moved slowly about the cottage touching odd things here and there, drawing the curtains to shut the night and prying eyes out and filling a hot water bottle for comfort. She changed into her pyjamas and then began assembling her evening meal of salad, smoked mackerel and a couple of spoons of basmati rice. She eschewed the option to have a cool drink, preferring once more to have tea and taking the whole lot through to the sitting room she sat at the dining table and ate in silence. It occurred to her that she hadn't heard another person's voice since she had arrived in Cornwall, that she hadn't shared a conversation with anyone since at least midday and that it was entirely possible that she might go quite mad with loneliness and boredom if she only had her thoughts to keep her company. Smiling to herself, she realised she was probably half way there already and that a week's silence would be no bad thing at all, and that this was a retreat from the world and from everything she was running away from.

There, she had finally admitted it. She was running away, but what from and why. She wasn't entirely sure and in this week she hoped to find out more about what had driven her to take flight, fearing that it was simply an act of defiance but recognising it was probably more of self preservation.

She stopped eating at this point, a forkful of food almost at her lips. The thoughts she had were rising unbidden and she was caught up amongst them unsure where to go or what to do now.

Stop it, she told herself, this is not the time for this sort of thinking, let's get on with it, there'll be time enough for that later, when I'm more settled and less frazzled.

Determinedly, she put the fork in her mouth and slid the food off and on to her tongue. She chewed slowly but deliberately, planning what to do next. Read and then bed perhaps.

Supper finished, plate and cutlery cleared to the kitchen and the washing up done and put away, it was the first time in the day that there was nothing specific to do or to be done.

Contemplating work was not appealing, but neither was the thought of a long evening ahead alone and with nothing to do but think. Already too many unwanted thoughts had surfaced, catching her unawares with their spontaneity and intensity. They frightened her and were voracious, an ever present threat to her fragile confidence. Now was not the time to allow them to run riot and cause the growing peace that had descended to take flight.

A book then; she'd brought some with her of course, a favourite Joanna Harris, the latest Alistair McCall Smith and a one by an author who was new to her. But she didn't fancy any of them. Drawn to the bookcase in the sitting room, she found the inevitable holiday cottage fare; the odd Maeve Binchy and Rosamunde Pilcher, both were favourite authors of hers in days past; a thriller or two, a genre which had never appealed, although she did admit occasionally to being a closet Dan Brown fan. There were books on bird watching, gardening and even a dictionary.

She'd just about given up hope of finding something to distract her, gloomily anticipating turning on the TV, when she spotted it. It was the title that captured her imagination first.

She picked it up off the shelf and turned it over expecting to be disappointed by the back blurb, but was pleasantly surprised to see that it was throwing down a sort of challenge, could it really be 'unusual and insightful' as was promised. Perhaps this was a sign of things to come and besides nothing else was appealing at the moment, so this had to do.

If necessary, she reasoned, she could always take a trip up to St Ives or into Penzance and pick up something else instead, or perhaps a few cheap DVD's to watch.

She decided to make yet another cup of tea.

It was almost as if her life span could be measured in teacups and mugs. Was this a three cup day or a ten cup day? The number of cups could potentially be divined by those who were interested in what sort of a day it had been. The higher the number, the greater the boredom or frustration, the lower the number the more likely she'd been out doing something reasonably interesting instead.

Idly she wondered whether she might have drunk the entire box by the end of the week, not that this worried her, she had camomile with her too, as well as bottles of Ginger Beer and other interesting things to drink. It's just that when she was particularly stressed or feeling unsure of herself, tea was the only thing that would do. It was the miracle cure as far as she was concerned and as long as she had tea to drink she knew that nothing too bad would happen.

Cup of tea in one hand, book in the other she climbed the stairs, turned the bed down and dimmed the lights. Reclining against the pillows she read the first line and was lost.

Chapter 2
Saturday

The bed was comfortable but unfamiliar as is the way with beds in other people's places or homes. It had none of the familiar ridges and hollows of her own bed, and being new was yet to develop its own. She revelled in the newness of it, feeling the down of the duvet and listening to it crackle in the way that only a feather filled one would do, the sheets felt silky smooth, probably M&S she thought, there were no bobbles of lint from over washing, there were no catches scratching unwary skin. Underneath the sheet she felt a cushioned mattress cover that gave the whole bed a feeling of sumptuousness and luxury far beyond anything she'd been expecting before she arrived.

She had chosen to sleep right in the middle, had cast the two extra pillows into the spare bedroom as un-necessary and it would save Margery, the owner, from having to wash and iron the pillow cases ready for the next guests. Her own pillow brought from home was at the bottom, the two pillows from the right hand side of the bed placed on top so that she had something comfortable to lean against as she drank tea, and she sat regally with a cup of tea placed on a spare book on top of the chair to her right and the curtains open. If she looked hard enough, she could just make out the sea, but the sky was overcast and it all seemed to merge together.

It wasn't her habit to sleep in the middle, normally she slept on the left side of the bed, she had been doing this for years even during all the time she'd slept alone. It felt risky and challenging to be in the middle and was probably something that had contributed to her not sleeping that well. It was if she hadn't slept at all, which was silly she knew, because she'd seen enough documentaries and read enough articles about sleep to realise that she had probably just woken up a lot instead. She certainly wouldn't feel as awake as she did right now if she'd not slept at all.

As Rosemary sat with tea in hand she suddenly realised it was Saturday and that there was a farmers market on in the village. Not knowing what time it was, she reached for her mobile phone which she had kept close just in case anybody had called overnight. Not that anyone ever did, even at home. Flicking it on, she was shocked to see it was ten thirty already, the market had started at ten and she wasn't sure when it was due to finish, was it twelve perhaps as it was at home? Resenting having to get out of something so comfortable, but determined not to miss out on a possible treat, she drained her cup and dragged herself into the bathroom to try out the newly fitted shower.

It worked perfectly; there was no running away to the furthest corner to escape something burning hot or too cold, just a perfect temperature almost immediately. True she had taken the shower head out of it's cradle and was pointing it away from her while she turned the mixer on, but still, it wasn't an experience she was often used to when she stayed away.

The water running over her body felt good, it splashed across her face, her breasts and her hips, gently rinsing the grime and sweat of the night away. Her hair was washed clean and conditioned and while that was working its magic, she washed her face and then soaped her body with shower gel, paying particular attention to her feet. She never knew why she paid so much attention to her feet, but she always did, as if she was recognising the vital role they played in her life, allowing her to walk or run at will, to just move about the world.

She let her hands drop and stood completely immersed in the stream of water from the shower, aware that she was doing things and becoming aware of things that had never occurred to her before. All these questions that kept rising up; silly things like, why did she always pay attention to her feet, what was going on, why is this happening, what is happening to her, was she going mad after all?

She became conscious of not moving and automatically raised her hands her to head to remove the conditioner from her hair as it would be sticky if she forgot to take it off and then she'd be uncomfortable all day. Turning the shower off she opened the cubicle door by pulling it towards her, it concertinaed inwards and she stepped out on to the dark blue shower mat that was awaiting just such an eventuality.

She stretched out reaching for one of the smaller towels which she wrapped turban style around her head to begin the process of drying her hair. She then pulled a larger towel from the rail and was disappointed to find that it was small, barely larger than a hand towel. It was the first thing she had to complain about and was glad she had brought a couple of large beach towels with her. The tiny towel was barely enough to cover part of her shoulders and it had been washed with fabric conditioner too, which meant it didn't dry her properly either. At home, Rosemary favoured over-large bath towels that were coarse to the touch and never had a hint of conditioner about them. She liked their rough feel and it helped to slough away the dead skin cells too.

Tiptoeing into the bedroom in a vain attempt to stop the trail of water droplets off her body, she walked round the bed to the chest of drawers, opened the third one down and reached in for the big blue beach towel; she left the pink one for when she went swimming later in the week.

Wrapping this firmly around herself she went back into the bathroom and proceeded with drying herself. Margery had asked her to give feedback and the one thing she would say would be about the towels. Guests should either bring their own or be provided with those of a decent size. She stopped herself, she was getting fierce, wound up, stressed and really there was nothing to be stressed about, it was only a towel and it was the only thing of note to offer an opinion on because the cottage surpassed expectations in so many other ways, others would be privileged to stay here.

She applied deodorant under her arms and then two different types of moisturiser to her face, a creamy serum around her mouth, noses and eyes in a half hearted acknowledgement of her age and then a lighter moisturiser over the rest of her face and neck. She had been using moisturiser since she was in her mid teens and it was this, coupled with the fact that she stayed out of the sun, that she attributed her complexion too. She didn't need make-up, in fact hadn't brought any with her. It was refreshing not to have to think about how other people might judge her based on her looks.

Here I can just be myself and no-one I come across will know any differently she thought.

Her wash complete, it was time to decide what to wear. Time was getting on and she didn't want to be late and miss all the fun at the market. Jeans and a simple tee-shirt seemed like the sensible choice, she didn't know if it was hot or cold out there and she'd wear trainers instead of summer shoes. Her hairdryer was in reach of the bed and she sat on the edge and dried her short thick hair. She was proud of her hair and had it cut regularly, she also had it coloured but it was to her natural colour so most people could never tell and that was the way she liked it.

Making her way to the kitchen with her empty cup, she decided to have breakfast first before heading out, recognising that if she didn't eat first, that she would probably get hungry while out and then end up eating something she didn't really want. Cereal was poured into the bowl and covered in milk and she leant against the sink to eat it, not wanting to sit down in case she decided not to get up again. She was eager to be off, to see the village she had ended up in and to find out whether the farmers market was anything like the ones at home.

Popping the bowl in the sink with a promise to herself to wash up later Rosemary made her way to the front door, stopping to pick up a key along the way. She debated whether the take a handbag or not and finally decided against it, stuffing notes and coins into her back pocket from her purse instead. Spotting a freebie lanyard from the last conference she was at in her bag she quickly clipped the house key to it and looped it over her neck. There, she was ready to go and had nothing to worry about carrying so her hands were free.

The walk to the village centre was longer than she thought it was going to be and she was grateful for only wearing the tee-shirt because it was hotter than she'd imagined. Instead of walking up the road as she had the previous evening she turned immediately left out of the cottage and headed along the lane, the visitors information book in the cottage promised that this would bring her out further along the road and perhaps closer to the pavements.

She saw no-one but did see even more blackberries and resolved once again to pick them; it appeared that there was a bumper harvest in the offing, enough for her and all the birds too and so she needn't worry about depriving them of essential food through the winter.

Rosemary remembered what her dad used to say, 'don't strip the whole branch, leave about half' that way, he explained, the birds would be OK too.

Memories of childhood and long late autumn evenings spent picking bilberries and blackberries in Wales and more recently of sloes and elderberries for tonics, syrups and liqueurs surfaced, bathing her in their innocence. Life somehow had seemed simpler then, easier and less full of the things unsaid and undone. She was wandering around the depths of her imagination and her memories; too late the present came flooding back to her and she found tears starting in her eyes.

No, I will not deal with this now and she brushed the tears away roughly and taking a huge breath brought to bear a strength of will she hadn't seen in herself for a long time.

The lane ended at the main road satisfyingly close to the pavement. It seemed that the village of Penmeor was long and thin, spread out along the roads length with little in the way of side streets and back streets. Rosemary spotted an alley running along the back of one row of houses on the other side of the road and wondered if it were possible to walk the whole length of the village from behind instead of from the main road. She thought that it might be nice to explore it another day, it would be more pleasant than walking on a main road, even if the main road is as quiet as this.

Rosemary took no time at all to reach the first of the two pubs that the information booklet had promised. The second was not much further on too. The centre of the village was not far away now and she could see people emerging from a hall laden down with baskets that have the tops of carrots and other vegetables showing. Anticipation quickened her step and in no time she was there on the threshold of a possible adventure.

The village hall was built with lottery funding, so said the plaque above the entrance proudly. The vestibule was full of notice boards, leaflets and books and all were clearly for sale to raise funds.

So, if I run out of things to read I can always come down here to replenish my stock she thought.

Rosemary also spotted the notice 'Internet and Laptop' and decided to find out more before she left.

Wandering into the main hall she could see that the farmers market was in full swing, if you could call half a dozen stalls, a few quiet patrons and the tea kiosk in full swing. Rosemary was so glad she had brought some money because she realised that she would have to buy something.

The first stall was all meat which she was avoiding for the week; the second was cheese and a cheerful chap in white coat and straw boater beamed broadly at her.

'Madam?'

She hadn't been called that in a long time and was momentarily startled. It was almost a question; she cast a glance over his goods with an appraising eye and spotted a blue cheese.

'Is that similar to Blue Vinney?' she enquired.

'Why don't you try it Madam' and he offered her a dish with some small squares handily pricked with cocktail sticks.

Popping a piece into her mouth, she heard him tell her that it was soft and not as tangy as Blue Vinney and found that she had to agree with him.

'I'll take a small round please' she said and handed over three pounds.

Carrying on around the room, the next two stalls look interesting, more meat and home made pies, but once again they were off the agenda because of her detox and the cheese she would save to take home.

The next stall was the source of the vegetables that everyone was walking out with. It was the longest table of the lot and had huge baskets of produce stacked up at the front as well as being laden all along the top. To the left were the roots, potatoes, carrots, onions and beetroots. To the right were the fruits, including apples, pears and a huge range of berries. Surprised to note that everything on the stall was in season, Rosemary reflected that this must be the product of working with the land instead of against it. There were no grapes, no oranges, and it all served to demonstrate that it was most likely locally grown and sourced.

In the baskets at the front were enormous sweet corn, broccoli and curly kale. But, she had already brought everything she needed with her and decided to buy a small handful of purple sprouting broccoli, just to show willing and it would be perfect slightly steamed with her salad that evening.

Sixty pence lighter she headed for the last two stalls. The first was home-made sauces and soup and on first glance she dismissed it as not appropriate, recognising that she had no real desire to cook while she was away. However, a closer look meant that she spied a pot of nettle and garlic soup, just enough for one person and found herself unable to resist, rationalising that nettles and garlic were great cleansers parting with one pound fifty in the process.

The man behind the stall was grateful, 'that's my favourite too' he said and smiled at her.

The last stall was the obligatory craft stall stuffed with out of shape knitted animals and cushion covers. There were colourful blankets and a myriad of tiny little key ring charms, all knitted of course. The woman manning the stall was ready to pounce. 'It's all pure wool' she stressed, running her hands over a blanket or two in the process. Murmuring an excuse Rosemary moved away before she could be persuaded into further sales conversation.

Finally there was the tea stall which was housed in the kitchen of the hall and which had two ladies behind it selling 'refreshments'; small iced biscuits, slices of large moist fruit cakes, tea and coffee. There was juice for the children, should any consent to show up and after ordering a cup of tea, Rosemary sat down at a table and started to watch what was going on about her.

She had been in the hall less than twenty minutes and already it was filling up. It was nearly midday and suddenly there was a rush on. Other people come in and the volume in the hall started to rise, people became animated and stall holders came to life. Old friends greeted each other warmly and acquaintances exchange pleasantries.

The buzz in the room was palpable and becoming more insistent by the minute. She sat transfixed by the energy that was rising and by the slow dance of the crowd that was growing. People wove around each other, this way and that, going from stall to stall, buying, selling and chatting. And all the while they were catching up with the gossip and imparting some of their own.

Snippets floated across to her, this person's daughter has got married and that person's grandson had an accident at school. The conversations were the same the world over but in this place it seemed they held more meaning. As she sat and listened Rosemary reflected that perhaps it was just that she had never really paid attention to life as other people live it before and that this was what made it seem somehow more real.

This is life she mused and in that moment realised she has never really entered into 'life' before. Perhaps this is what I sought, perhaps coming here was meant to be.

Suddenly the noise level dropped and she glanced round to see what had happened. There was no reduction in the number of people in the room, but it was definitely quieter. A woman had walked in with a small child in tow and pushing a modern pram high up from the floor with the baby facing its mother gurgling quietly.

She realised it was the young woman who waved to her when she arrived the day before and prepared to smile a greeting in acknowledgement but then noticed that the woman had her head down and was looking at no-one. People were definitely watching her though, they were interested, but not in a positive way. The feeling in the room had changed to something like that of the pack turning on a wounded mate trying to drive it out and protect the rest of them from predators. The hall had acquired a feeling of discord to it and she noticed that as people sensed this they started to turn away concluding their business quickly and then leaving. The noise level had also dropped even further but this time it was because the room was emptying.

Rosemary watched as the young woman quickly made purchases of vegetables and fruit, meat and some pies. It was apparent that the child, a girl she could now tell, was starting to feel the tension in the room and was becoming fractious pulling at her mothers arm and insisting they leave 'now!'. Without saying a word, the woman turned the pram around and left the hall; barely anything had been said to her or by her beyond the business transactions. Unlike everyone else, no one had said hello or stopped for a chat.

Curious about what had just happened and knowing that there were so many questions to ask it had been over so quickly, in about five minutes all told. What on earth could that woman have done to be the focus of such a huge amount of animosity? Clearly she was local; someone that wasn't would never have attracted that much attention.

By now though the room was starting to fill once again and the noise levels rose accordingly. Friends were once more talking to friends and people seemed happier. Finishing off her tea she rose to leave and once again caught the eye of the man behind the soup stall. He smiled, and she smiled back, a small acknowledgement that it was OK for her to be there.

On her way out she stopped at the information desk to ask about Internet access. Oh yes, she was told, the centre was open until three most days and there was wireless access at a cost of one pound for each hour of use. She could, if she wanted, bring her laptop down and deal with her email then. If she wanted!

The village was, as she'd already noted long and shallow with a row of houses of varying types and sizes on each side of both road and pavement. It wasn't what you would call attractive either with its grey stone and slate and a fair amount of pebble dash on what had been, or perhaps still were, council houses. They all looked moody and disconsolate.

Rosemary wondered what they would look like when the weather was really bad. Perhaps a good dose of bright sunshine would bring them to life. There were few signs of life about the place and apart from the bustle in the farmers market there was almost no one about. Although there were a few dozen cars in the car park they were probably outliers coming in to get stocked up. The village stores were almost deserted and she'd not really seen in on the way into the village because the door seemed to be facing the wrong way to be spotted. Close by was the post office and it too seemed to lie in the wrong direction for spying on and she only caught sight of it because a red post office van was drawn up outside.

Just then a small group of children made their way round the corner. The oldest was admonishing the younger ones, telling them to be careful and keep away from the road; she was clearly taking her duties in loco parentis very seriously and Rosemary smiled imagining herself at the same age. She had seen enough family videos to know that she had been bossy and would definitely have been ordering her siblings about had she had any. The group passed by on the other side of the road and made for the entrance to the village hall. They were off to the farmers market and perhaps a glass of squash and a biscuit.

As they passed out of sight, she dismissed them from her mind and turned her thoughts once more to the young woman she had seen earlier. Thinking back over the events in the hall Rosemary recalled that although the woman hadn't acknowledged anyone and that neither had she been acknowledged there was nothing about her manner which suggested that she had been bothered by the reception she had received. It was almost as if she had barely registered there was anyone else around. Her business had been concluded swiftly and she'd left. When she'd raised her hand in greeting yesterday there had been no expectation of anything other than a friendly smile or wave in return. Rosemary was briefly ashamed of the way she had dismissed the small family the day before and determined to be more open and friendly if given another opportunity to do so.

Her thoughts returned to the village, there was no point in wondering what was going on with the young woman, it would be mere speculation.

It was clear from both sight of the village and the guidebook that this area had once been the scene of a thriving tin mining industry and the cottage she was staying in was testimony to the success of the ventures. Its industrial heritage was the reason for the way the village presented itself now. This was no quaint and picturesque place, unlike Dorset, which she thought of as the milkmaid county, all apple cheeks and rosy prettiness. It was bleak; there was a sense of clinging to the edge of the land holding on tight to prevent being swept away into the wide Atlantic Ocean. In many ways it reminded her of the Lake District as there were few trees around, and those that clung on were either being tended in gardens or were small straggly things bent double by the frequent winds that blew. That in itself was its own kind of beauty though, the wide expanse of fields and moor setting down their feet in the cliffs that overhung the beaches.

All around her the silence was deafening. Once again this was not a silence without sound; rather this was the silence of no people. There were no dogs barking, no sound of chatter behind hedges or walls; there was no music coming from open windows. Only the occasional car driving past gave an indication that there were still people alive on earth.

For one moment she had a picture of being the last person left, and being trapped in Penmeor forever, with no one to talk to and no bright spark to lighten her loneliness. Shaking her head, she dismissed the thought and focused once more on the locality. Where did people work these days? Did they go into Penzance; were they part of the burgeoning tourist trade? What exactly had taken over when the tin mining stopped? What about the children? That there were some was evidenced by the largish village school she had seen opposite the village hall, but there were none in evidence again and apart from the small group that had just entered the village hall and the two from yesterday, she couldn't recall seeing any others at all. She knew that in some rural parts of the country there were massive drug problems fuelled by the lack of activities and jobs, she wondered if this was the fate of a village like Penmeor too and supposed that she would never really know for she was only passing by and wouldn't be staying to see into the heart of the village and its people.

Perhaps I could go to the pub. She wondered out loud and then stopped realising she was talking to herself.

The pub was definitely the place to see what a village was really like, but she rejected the idea almost as soon as she'd thought it as foolish. She didn't want to be pestered by those who didn't know her and who might assume that if she were on her own she'd be game for anything. Pubs and women on their own didn't mix; a bit like villages in general she thought. You would always be viewed with suspicion if you were a single woman living alone in a village, people assuming that you were odd if you didn't have a man in tow.

By now, she had reached the lane that would take her off the main road and back towards home. 'Home', there was a word to conjure with and she was surprised that it had come so readily to her when thinking about returning to the cottage. She wondered at this and then realised it was because it was homely and so felt cosy and safe. There was no threat there and once she closed the door it represented security too. It was sometimes astonishing how quickly one could feel 'at home' somewhere and it probably had something to do with the quality of the people that lived there before her own arrival she supposed; after all it was people that made a home, not possessions. She thought of her little apartment in Dorset, that was home too, it was secure and safe, somewhere to retreat to when the world became too much and she hoped that when visitors came to see her, that they felt 'at home' as well. Perhaps home was defined by the memories that were locked into the fabric of a building, good memories building up a layer of positivity that others felt when they entered the place and negative memories creating something you wanted to get away from as soon possible.

She recalled a house she had once visited as a prospective buyer; even before she entered the house she knew she could never live there. It was perfect on paper but it exuded malice. Even the garden which should have been rich and abundant was dank and slimy. She hadn't made it beyond downstairs, knowing that nothing on earth would persuade her to visit the upper rooms. She had made excuses about being late for another appointment to the estate agent and the owners and was shocked to realise she was shaking when she sat back in the car again. That house had haunted her dreams for weeks after that, every one ending in the same way, a long wail of absolute despair coming from the bedroom at the back whose door was locked and bolted. At the time, she had simply thought her imagination, overactive at the best of times, had simply surpassed itself; but looking back now, she couldn't be so sure.

As she walked, she looked much more closely at the hedgerow and walls, realising that there was far more going on than the ripening of blackberries. At the base were mixtures of dandelion, thistle and goatsbeard, in the cracks between stones appeared ribwort, ferns and scabious. Every so often there was a drift of hydrangea gone wild and huge banks of overgrown fuchsias escaped from the gardens beyond. Of course there were the nettles and dock leaves too, as well as an infinite seeming variety of grasses, each area a small environment in its own right. And over all, the blackberries, great shiny clusters of tiny berries, glossy black and brimming with juice. Perfect for picking, but she had no bags and once again promised herself the treat of coming back to harvest what nature had to offer.

Soon she was back and once her small purchases were safely installed in the fridge she decided to make a hot drink and to sit for while before making any decisions about what to do next. It was well after one o'clock and the walk back had taken longer than she had anticipated, probably because she kept being distracted by the sights and sounds of her journey. With a drink in one hand she gathered up a blanket and settled herself at one end of the sofa, with her back in the corner and her feet stretched out along its length, she felt herself relax. She sipped the golden liquid and with each mouthful relaxed further still. This was definitely the life, it couldn't get much better than this; tea and a whole week stretching ahead of her that didn't involve her being at anyone's beck and call, she could just be.

Before she'd arrived she had thought a lot about what she might do while she was away; there was Penzance of course and St Ives. Mousehole was another option and there were some lovely houses and gardens too. But now that she was here, the thought of leaving her sanctuary, even for a few hours, seemed faintly ridiculous. She didn't have to be a tourist, even if she was one. Just because she was in a part of the world rarely visited before did not mean she had to conform to expectations and spend her time busily rushing from one sight to the next without really appreciating where she actually was.

A week, getting to know the feel of this village was really what she wanted more than anything else. She didn't have to go anywhere and the car could quite happily stay parked up for a week. If she needed anything there was always the local store.

No, I'll stay put, she thought. She drank the remaining tea from her cup and put it on the side table, pulling the blanket that draped across the back of the sofa over her she snuggled further down and closed her eyes, there was nothing a short nap wouldn't sort out. Shortly her breathing lengthened and deepened and she was asleep.

Rosemary woke suddenly, the little cottage was quiet but something had startled her and brought her back to the present. The light outside had changed and she surmised it must be around five o'clock. The blanket had slipped off her sometime during the afternoon and she was cold, her feet especially felt leaden and numb.

Pushing herself up slowly she was aware of a headache forming; so much for a nourishing afternoon nap. Sleep was obviously something that was needed; she'd slept so badly for months now that she wasn't at all surprised that it had overtaken her.

Despite the headache, she felt lighter and aware that her body was shifting its shape, moving away from the tight, tense closed in self she had exhibited for months and becoming more open and freer somehow. It felt good, her muscles were beginning to forgive her and although they were aware of being exercised by the walking, they relished the prospect of being used for their purpose instead of held in check.

In the kitchen, she hesitated over the kettle. Did she really want more tea or something else instead? The fridge contained a selection of Ginger Beer, one of her favourites; she had no wine or alcohol with her, simply fizzy mineral water, a bottle of squash, the ginger beer, tea bags and camomile. If none of those sufficed she would have water from the tap.

Ginger beer called to her and she poured herself a long glass, sugar rushed to her head as she drank and it felt cool against her throat. She drained the glass quickly and poured a second one, this time taking it into the sitting room with her. She was now wide awake and had no intention of going back to sleep, the headache that had threatened had receded as soon as she had started to move around, so she sat once more this time with her feet stretched towards the unlit stove.

She'd been dreaming, of that she was certain. Half remembered fragments came back to her as she sat; a man shouting, a young girl with ringlets and rosebud lips and a telephone box on a street corner; each one seemingly complete in themselves but hinting at something bigger.   She'd seen the telephone box before but struggled to recall where it was.

Letting her mind wander, she drew her eyes inward and allowed the memories to float back. Ah, yes that was it. Edinburgh, outside the station on Waverley Bridge, it was the first time she had met James.

Chapter 3

She was late and it was raining. Scrabbling around in her briefcase and realising she'd left her umbrella behind did nothing to improve her mood. The journey had been foul, it had taken longer than she'd thought and she'd been blocked into a corner by a man who kept offering her sweets and leering at her suggestively. She had feigned sleep in an effort to discourage his attentions and would have moved seats if she'd thought another might be available somewhere.

Reaching her journeys end, she was relieved to be able to leave the close, confined space behind and feeling a soft breeze on her face as she started up the slope out of the station, her spirits began to lift despite the rain. Her pace quickened and a glance at her watch confirmed her worst fears, she was very late indeed and the interviews might soon be over. She started to jog along, not caring that she would turn up dishevelled and hot, bothered only by time. Rounding the corner at the top of the ramp too quickly she collided at full tilt with a man who was equally distracted and not paying attention to his whereabouts and doing exactly the same thing she was but in reverse.

'I'm so sorry', they both apologised at the same time.

He offered her a hand up and she took it gratefully, not sure of her footing as she was shaking and disorientated.

'Is there anything I can do to help?'

His voice was soft with a slight Scottish burr, suggesting although he'd be born somewhere north of the border he had, in fact spent more time away from his home country than in it.

'I'm on my way to an interview and I'm very late'.

She looked down at her clothes, not only wet now but dusty and her tights had laddered, not exactly the picture of efficient professionalism she had intended.

'Can I get you a taxi perhaps?'

He was solicitous and concerned and she appreciated the gesture, aware that he was making an effort on her behalf.

'That would be great, if you have time'.

Holding her arm he guided her across Waverley Bridge to the telephone boxes that overlooked the gardens. He guided her into one, out of the rain, while he opened the door to another. Quickly dialling the number of the company he used regularly, he spoke rapidly into the receiver, giving directions and then put the phone down.

He opened the door to her telephone box, 'they'll be here shortly and I've put it on my account'.

She opened her mouth to object, and he held his hand up.

'It's the least I can do'.

Accepting, she nodded acquiescence, her normal feminist principles disarmed by her pain and his kindness.

'Look, I really have to go; I have a train to catch. Is there anything else I can help you with?'

He was looking at his watch as he said it and she was conscious that he had been as pressed for time as she was, they wouldn't have had their accident otherwise.

'No, nothing, thank you, thanks for your help, you've already done too much'. She smiled at him and her face was transformed.

He was moved to do something more, but didn't know what was appropriate, reaching into his coat pocket he brought out a handkerchief and a business card, he handed them to her saying 'this is for your knee, you can clean it up in the taxi perhaps and this is my card in case there is anything else you think of'.

She murmured her thanks and at that moment a black cab drew up.

'Mr Edwards?' the driver stuck his head out the window.

'Oh, it's not for me, it's for my friend ...' he looked at her quizzically, waiting for her to supply her name;

'Rosemary' she responded.

'Rosemary' he repeated to the driver.

'I've spoken to Jack and it's on my account'. He opened the door for her to step inside and she sat down gratefully. Shutting the door firmly, he tapped on the driver's side window and gave thumbs up. The taxi driver turned back to her and asked 'where to then?'

'The University please', she turned back to the road side and realised Mr Edwards had gone, to get his train obviously.

James watched the taxi disappear round the corner on to Princes Street and then shaking his head as if to clear the last ten minutes from it carried on across the road and down the ramp into Waverley Station. He'd missed his train and would just have to wait for the next, his meeting could wait and he deserved a coffee to recover his composure.

The interview did not go well, not only was she late, but she didn't have time to clean up before being taken by the faculty administrator straight in to see the Dean. Apologies did not seem to go down well, nor did excuses about the train being late and her accident elicited no sympathetic hearing, just a nod of the head and an acceptance that even in this short space of time, she had already disappointed.

In short order she was back at the station, she had barely been in Edinburgh two hours and her experience had not been positive, she thought that it would be better if she never visited the city again. Edinburgh, with its vast and extended history, its architecture and culture, didn't stand a chance against the determination she felt never to set foot in that place again. It was, it turned out, the only time she ever visited the city and thereafter, every time someone mentioned its name she would shudder and recount her tale of woe, insistent that the city hadn't wanted her there and that it had merely been telling her so.

She returned to Dorset dispirited. At twenty she was still in her home county. Many of her friends were now spread across the nation, in various centres of learning and were living a life so far removed from her own that it seemed they were of different planets. When they returned home, there was less and less to connect and bind them to each other and she, who had chosen to work instead of carry on her education after A levels felt like she was being left behind, a relic of some long forgotten childhood, which would only be indulged on high days and holidays. They drifted apart and she started to make a life separate from them with new friends being offered up in the form of work colleagues.

She had found a job at eighteen working for the local authority as an administrative assistant in the Personnel department. Being naturally tidy and organised and with a good head for logic, she quickly rose through the ranks to become one of two personal assistants to the Head of Personnel, the youngest person to hold such a title within the entire council.

She had been encouraged by her employer to start training for her Institute of Personnel Management qualifications, the intention being that at some point, in the long distant future and when enough of the senior staff had either retired or died, that she might fill their place and become a Personnel Manager. Every month or so, she scoured the papers and the trade journals to see what, if anything, there might be open to her outside of the small rural county she had thus far spent her entire life in.

The job in Edinburgh had been perfect, requiring someone with her mixture of experience and naivety to become part of a management training scheme that the University was piloting. But it was clearly not meant to be and she proceeded to set her sights lower preferring to remain in the anonymity of the job she already had, working as hard and conscientiously as ever, but without the same enthusiasm.

Although her experience of Edinburgh had not been a wholly positive one, she was grateful to the man who had come to her rescue, ignoring the fact that he had been as much to blame for their accident as she had. On her return, she laundered the handkerchief, ironed it carefully and using the address on the business card, had returned it to him with a card by way of thanks. He had written back shortly after to say he had received the card and was pleased she was OK, but sorry to hear she hadn't got the job. And slowly, over the following months, they fell into an easy rhythm of letter writing, each letter slightly more exposing than the last, each revealing more of themselves than they had perhaps intended.

He learnt that she was twenty years old, that her birthday was in June and that she was a Cancerian. That she aspired to be a Personnel Manager, had three 'A' levels in English Literature, Sociology and Psychology.

He heard about her nights out with friends, how she disliked living at home with her parents, but hated the idea of sharing with other girls even more. She was saving for a deposit for her own home and had a cat called Angus.

She learnt that his name was James, he was twenty six and that he was an accountant just finishing off his final qualifications. He was Scottish and from Edinburgh which was why he was often sent to deal with Scottish clients, but had lived most of his life in Birmingham with his Mother who was a widow. He too was saving for somewhere to live, but it had to be the right place, because he couldn't see the point of sharing either. He didn't have any pets, but rather liked the idea of a owning a dog or two and he'd call at least one of them 'Jim'.

It is on such small niceties that relationships are built; they encourage an expectation of similarity of purpose, values and ethos; whilst in reality they are only surface mounted and do not run deep.

Over time, it became apparent to both of them that they should meet up again, if only to say 'hello' and to enjoy some time spent together. Underlying this agreement was a hope that each of them had, that they had found 'the one'. It was neither spoken nor inferenced in any of their communications, each believing that some magic would cause whatever was supposed to 'happen', to happen.

Both were shy, it had taken a lot for Rosemary to put her head above the parapet and apply for a job at the other end of the country from where she lived; and it had taken James by surprise when he had offered Rosemary his handkerchief and business card. Privately, both felt that this was 'meant to be', that the gods had decreed that they should bump into each other on Waverley station and that as a result their relationship was destined for great things.

However, as those who have been through divorce know well, this does not encourage exploration of those things that make a relationship real, such as real values and ethics, having a mutual understanding and agreement that it is OK to be an individual as well as part of a couple. In a way, they were typical of their generation, looking at the generalities of life, without looking deeper and beyond the surface presentation.

They met for the second time, in London, he rushing across the city on the tube from Charing Cross, to meet her train at Waterloo. It had been six months since they'd last met and they were cautious and solicitous of each other, stumbling over words and sentences in their nervousness.

She thought he was the epitome of the ideal husband; going somewhere with a career that would keep her in a lifestyle to which she felt she could easily become accustomed.

In turn, he thought she was a china doll, something to wrap up carefully and look after for the precious thing it was. Neither saw the other as they really were; he gauche and controlling and she naive and rebellious. If they had, perhaps things might not have gone the way they did, but too often in life we see only what we want to see and not what is really in front of us.

They both concluded that the meeting went well, that the other had matched their expectations and that here was indeed 'the one'. Curiously, neither of them referred to this, fearing that if they mentioned their hopes the other might be frightened off and run away.

With the benefit of hindsight it was obvious that they were given lots of opportunities to change minds, ask questions and explore options; but neither of them did. Although they were both thinking about a lot of things, they were reluctant to question, worried that it might cause a rift of some description, so each maintained their role and showed the other only that side of themselves which confirmed the assumptions already made.

The courtship gathered pace and they were meeting regularly now, at least once every two to three weeks, and writing almost daily. Both sets of parents complained of mounting phone bills and privately both Rosemary and James were looking forward to moving out and into their own home for a bit of peace and quiet.

One question which it was necessary to broach was the question of where they would live when they eventually married. James favoured Edinburgh he longed to return to the city of his birth and had an opportunity to do so with his accountancy practice which would be happy to be relieved of the expenses he presented each time he visited a client. Rosemary was adamant though, she would not live in Edinburgh, but neither did she want to live in Dorset. She wanted what her school fellows had already achieved, freedom from the yoke of home and parents and she perceived that this could only happen if she were well away from any influence they might have through their physical presence.

James's mother was unhappy about her son leaving home and brought familial pressure to bear, how could he leave her all alone now that his father was dead, who would look after her and help her tend the garden? Her constant concern was that she would die without anyone ever knowing and that she would lie, a corpse, in her sitting room un-noticed for weeks. Putrefying and disintegrating, destroying the carpet that had cost so much money to have fitted.

In the end James capitulated, they would stay in Birmingham. Rosemary was happy because she would be out of Dorset and into a big city with all the promise of a more exciting social life and cultural adventure, James's mother was happy because she would have a daughter as well as son to pander to her needs, Rosemary's parents were secretly relieved, fearing that they would be expected to visit regularly if she had stayed close to home and secretly James was pleased because it gave him a chance to be magnanimous towards his bride-to-be, showing her he cared and that he would always look after her. The only nose out of joint was his accountancy practice which would still have to fund his monthly trips to Edinburgh. On the whole though, it was a pretty satisfactory result.

Chapter 4
Saturday

She had sat for too long, her legs were stiff and uncomfortable and they needed to move so she returned to the kitchen and once more filled the kettle with water thinking over those first heady months; how much promise there had been, what hopes they had both had. It was just a shame that they hadn't shared them with each other. One of their problems she realised now had been that they were both too caught up in their own needs to recognise a need to share their partners'. In fact, singular of purpose was a phrase she now thought apt. But their purposes were so far apart that they didn't even see them.

She placed the kettle carefully on to the base and turned it on, reminded as she did so of a talk she had heard recently about health and safety law and how to apply the need for PAT testing, a kettle was one thing which would need testing annually and she wondered if this was something she ought to mention in her notes to Margery at the end of the week. Then she realised that Margery was a professional in this game, she already had one cottage and probably knew more about what was required and what wasn't that she could ever hope to learn. Dismissing the idea she returned to the act of making tea.

There was something almost mystical about tea she thought, she preferred to add the milk first because this helped to reduce the strength of the brew. She didn't like strong tea, preferring milder mixes such as Earl Grey with its bergamot and Lady Grey with its lemony tang. It was the latter she had brought with her to Cornwall and as she popped a tea bag into the mug she had placed ready she wondered what it was that had caused her to start drinking it. She realised it was James's mother, with her pretentious airs and graces who had introduced her to this fine brew not long after they had married.

There was always something to be grateful for she mused.

She returned to the sitting room and drew the blanket over her once more, allowing her legs to fall free from their hips and down to the rug below. She settled a cushion behind her and lay back once more nursing a mug in both hands. It would be time to eat soon and she was looking forward to such a simple activity. At home, she always felt that she never had enough time to prepare meals, caught up in the work of the day until evening and then finding that she was eating late and then having to go to bed too soon for her meal to have digested. One of the nicest things about being here like this was freedom from the routine she had managed to create.

She wondered briefly about turning on the television, there was bound to be something on that would distract her from her thoughts; she dismissed it, in all likelihood she would just get annoyed and start shouting at the screen.

Rosemary reached for her book instead. The previous night she had managed to read about a quarter before turning off the light and slipping down to sleep.

As she read, she noticed similarities between herself and the two main characters. They were both acting out roles, roles that were determined by their status and place in society, she too had spent a lifetime acting out a role; the only difference between her and the characters though was that they were aware of doing so and had entered into the contractual obligations that their role dictated almost willingly, challenging society at the same time as conforming to it.

She on the other hand had not noticed she was in a play, a play called 'life' to be sure, but a play nonetheless. She had not entered into the role willingly and she hadn't even been aware she was playing it until a short time ago. She wondered whether this was the reason that the book had appealed to her, perhaps it had called to her from the bookshelf, speaking to a part of her that was buried deep but that could still hear the demand to be unleashed.

Reading until about seven o'clock Rosemary then checked her phone to be sure of the time and was both relieved and disappointed to note that no one had attempted to contact her. Did anyone care, she thought, where she was or what she was doing? Pushing the blanket aside and turning down the page of the book she closed it with a sigh.

Oh the problems we create for ourselves she thought.

In the kitchen she gathered together the ingredients for her evening meal, the same as the previous evening but replacing the mackerel with tuna this time. No meat was going to pass her lips this week, of that she was determined, and if she hadn't been aware of needing some protein she would not have brought the fish either, preferring instead to have just rice and salad.

There was a fly buzzing round and while she waited for the rice to cook she placed her salad plate and fish in the empty cupboard above the drainer for there was no fly screen to place over the food. As soon as the rice was boiled, she drained it and cooled it a little with fresh water before adding it to the retrieved meal.

Carrying this and cutlery into the sitting room she sat and faced the wall while she ate at the dining table. It was, she felt an entirely unsatisfactory view for an evening meal and resolved to change chairs so that she had at least a partial view out of the window for the next time she ate.

She ate quickly and carefully, she was neat in her movements and ensured her plate was cleared completely before returning it to the kitchen. Constant reminders over the years from both parents and James about the 'starving in Africa' had ensured she never added more to her plate than she was able to eat and she'd become a master at calculating portions when cooking for dinner guests. This meant of course that there were never any leftovers for cooking up the next day.

The making and consumption of her meal had taken a little under forty minutes altogether and so it was still early. She was faced with the dilemma of the TV again, should she succumb or stick to her guns. Sticking to her guns she reached once more for her book, but was startled by a strident announcement from her phone announcing she had received a message. The sound was discordant and at odds with the silence and for a moment she sat, shocked, unsure about what to do.

Flicking the phone on she read the message, it was just one line 'are you OK?'

Somehow the lack of a capital A at the start irritated her beyond measure, why do people do it! She re-read the message trying to fathom the meaning behind it; a face rose up before her and she realised that there probably was no meaning behind it that she had to work out, there was no underlying comment or statement or question that had to be divined before an answer could be given.

'Yes' she texted back, she hesitated before pressing send, realising that such a bald statement could be potentially hurtful. She added a 'x' to remove the sting and pressed send, trusting that the recipient would understand.

The text message had thrown her, although she was ok with her solitude, she was still a product of the society from which she had been bred, one that dictated that to have worth as a human being meant that you had a group of people around you that cared and were concerned for your welfare, in short you had friends and family. She was, sometimes she felt, without either.

She could no longer settle to her book, the intricacies of a life lived in a role in France were providing no interesting diversion, she was unsettled and fractious and could barely sit still. Outside it started to rain, she could hear it through the open window, a light drizzle at first and then great drops bouncing off the guttering and onto the ground beneath.

She would have liked to go for a walk, but was deterred by the thought of being wet as well as depressed - that would be no way to end the first full day of her week away. So she did what most people do in this situation, she turned on the TV and channel hopped for the next hour half hoping to find something that would absorb her and found nothing of interest at all. In the end she decided to retire to bed, beaten into submission by the evening and feeling that maybe coming away had not been such a great idea after all.

She made camomile tea with honey and took two ibuprofen tablets because her leg had started to ache, carrying her book she made her way to bed and placed herself securely back in the middle of the bed and drank deeply.   She hoped that the camomile tea would have the effect of soothing her and quietening her brain, unfortunately it did neither. But it did warm her through and she was eventually able to sleep.

Chapter 5
Sunday

She woke early but had no idea what the time was as she'd left her phone downstairs the night before. The cottage was still and quiet and there was no sound outside, not even of birds singing. She made her way carefully downstairs and flicked her phone on, 'less than 15% battery still remaining' was the warning notice so she checked the time, 7.05 am and then plugged the charger in and left the phone to its own devices.

She made a cup of tea and carried it upstairs to bed with her. Climbing back in Rosemary reflected that she'd never had so much tea in bed since she'd first got married. Back then James had been eager to bring it to her, to cosset her and care for her.

It's funny how our lives changed over the years, and how our roles changed too.

Stopping herself from going any further, she finished her drink and snuggled back down underneath the duvet, pulling it up close around her ears in case a dragon should swoop down and bite them off. She smiled at her childhood memory.

Surprisingly, given the evening she'd had the day before she was feeling good. In fact the word that was more appropriate was hopeful. Yes, that's right, hopeful. She stretched out like a starfish trying to get arms and legs into each corner of the bed, claiming it as her own territory again and acknowledging how good it felt to be alive.

Sunday stretched ahead of her and she was full of anticipation about the walk she might take. The book she was reading had taken on a new meaning too and she was now intrigued about what might happen to the characters; would they each achieve their goals? The similarities to her own situation were not completely lost on Rosemary and probably accounted for why the book had appealed so much.

She had no desire to venture out of the village, in fact no desire to venture far from the cottage if truth be told. Somehow it was fitting that the world fitted into just a couple of miles or so. It had shrunk to accommodate her and her needs as she had shrunk as a person over the years.

As she lay, she reflected on what she had become and with a shock realised that she was simply the product of someone else's imagination.

Where had Rosemary disappeared to and who was this imposter that now took her place.

Even now when she looked in the mirror she barely recognised the face that looked back at her, somehow it wasn't what she expected to see. She didn't mean the age thing, that was inevitable and came to us all in the end and she accepted that actually she looked good, and very young, for her age; no, it was more that the person she saw wasn't her, it was someone else. The person she thought she should see would be different somehow, but Rosemary found it hard to imagine what that face might look like.

She rolled over, frustrated and pulled the duvet even further up around her ears and closed her eyes and wept. Long hot salty tears coursed down her face as she thought of the opportunities missed, the lessons never learned, the woman she never became and most of all for the children she never had. Her sobs deafened her, but she was unable to stop.

All her life she had feared that if she ever started crying she would never stop, that the wellspring of tears would defeat her and overwhelm her and that she would cry her way to her grave. She felt the losses of her life so keenly and cried harder.

In an odd way though, she realised it felt good to cry, she had never allowed herself this luxury, knowing instinctively that her parents who rarely expressed emotion of any description would be unable to help her cope, and so she had bottled everything in, not letting it out, for fear of upsetting or hurting those around her and simply in the process, hurting herself even more.

The realisation that it felt good to cry reduced the flow of tears and eventually they seemed to stop. Gulping and gasping for air, she pulled her hand across her snotty, wet face. She reached under the pillow for the tissues she had placed there, just in case she had needed to blow her nose. She realised that the salt had made her face itchy and dry and as she rubbed she became aware too of a constant trickle of tears still running from her eyes, she obviously wasn't done yet.

Her nose had run so much that she could no longer breathe and it became necessary to sit up and blow. She blew, hard, and then again and felt immediately better. Suddenly she started laughing.

God, if only James could see me now she thought he'd be mortified.

She was still crying, but she was laughing too; unsure which was which, all she knew was that it felt like a huge weight had been lifted from her back and perceiving she was being given another chance to take a different path. Never again, would she keep her emotions to herself, if she needed to cry she reasoned, it was for a purpose and she'd bloody well cry. Laughter erupted again and she was delighted by her own revelation, figuring that if she had come this far then she could go anywhere she damn well felt like.

Rosemary decided that more tea was needed, it was, she thought after all hot, sweet tea that is said to be good for shock victims and she had certainly shocked herself. In the kitchen she realised she had no sugar, so substituted honey instead, promising to get a small bag when she went out for her walk later that day. Once again, she climbed the stairs with her mug and once again she climbed in to the very middle of the bed. Such small triumphs she thought, they were the stuff of change for she had recognised, however slightly, that change was afoot and now that it had started it was not about to allow its progress to be halted. Briefly, she wondered if there was something in the water and then surmised that it was simply the magic of the cottage doing its work.

Eventually lying in bed became too much and a strong need to get up, get dressed and get out overcame her. After showering and dressing she was finally ready to face the day by eleven. A quick bowl of cereal and she was off and out.

The day was disappointingly grey, she had half expected it to be bright and sunny to reflect the momentous events of her morning but it was not to be and nature was, it seemed, not sharing in her enthusiasm for life.

The mist was low and promised to get lower still, it threatened rain too although the wind had dropped and was barely fluttering the very edges of the shrubs as she walked by. She had turned left down the lane again. It was a quieter route to the village and the crossroads and she intended to walk as far as the sea this time, determined to get to the cliffs, if not the beach.

In the back pocket of her jeans were a couple of plastic food bags for blackberries, there was no way she was going to miss out on the harvest this time. As she trotted along, she paid attention to where the best bushes lay knowing that she would pick them on the way back, to save her having to carry them in both directions. The abundance of the growth suggested that no-one else had started picking yet and hopefully no-one would beat her to her source that day either.

She crossed the road and strode confidently out on to the lane beyond, feeling sure of her way after her walk when she had first arrived. Plenty of cars passed her in both directions and she assumed that they were going down to the hamlet and rows of cottages that were indicated on the map, although she had to admit that if that were indeed the case, then the villagers were a very busy lot because she had seen more cars than she had heard on the main road in all the time she had been in the cottage thus far.

Greyness was descending fast and a light mist was rolling in but she was determined to carry on to the end of the lane. She needed to see the sea, to have at least a glimpse of what lay beyond the fields in front of the cottage.

It was fortunate that she had put on a light waterproof jacket because she could feel droplets of water on her face and doing the jacket up she realised it was a little too small, regretfully she admitted to having gained a pound or two since she had bought it and just allowed it to ride up over her hips and settle on her waist; at least her top half would remain dry even if her legs and bum got wet. She pulled the hood up and fastened it tightly. She probably looked like little orphan Rosie and the image made her laugh out loud.

Other walkers looked at her strangely as they passed, seeing only a woman with a strange gleam in her eye and a big smile on her face, cheerily saying hello despite the dampness of the day and the gloom of the mist that surrounded everything.

She carried on buoyed by her lightness of being, she felt as if she had been released from a cage of her own creation and was finally being able to spread her wings for the first time ever. As she walked she allowed her arms to rise up to shoulder height, testing them for strength and aerodynamics. Perhaps she could fly after all; all she needed was a little lift underneath.

The breeze gathered momentum and rushed over the top of her arms and below, she loved its silky soft feel across the exposed skin of her wrists and hands and impulsively took her jacket off despite the mist. Tying it around her waist and clad now only in a tee-shirt and jeans she once more raised her arms as if to fly and experienced an adrenaline rush as the breeze quickened around her upper arms, tingling and tickling as it went. Her hair whipped back and forwards, into her eyes and out of them again, she was completely unaware of it but they sparkled.

More walkers passed her by amazed by the woman they saw before them, she must be quite mad, but she was obviously happy. In fact the feeling was one of joy and it came upon her slowly, creeping up from behind before announcing itself and she laughed out loud again and started to run into the wind, daring it to raise her up off the ground.

She stopped, breathless, and smiled.

This is how it feels to be happy she thought and oh how I've missed it.

Sliding her arms into her jacket she put it back on, realising that she had become a little cold and then carried on with the walk.

Her flight, if you could call it that, had taken her beyond her previous walk and she was into brand new sights and sounds. There were more cars in both directions and several times she had to stop and settle back against the stone walls to allow them to pass by. The number of walkers too seemed to be increasing, clearly there was something down here beyond the hamlet and the houses and she was determined to find out what it was.

The mist was closing in fast and it probably wasn't a mist any longer, more of a fog. Then a sound stopped her, long and deep; it was a foghorn. She'd only ever heard them in films or on TV documentaries, she'd never heard one in real-life and the sound was every bit as mournful as Hollywood and the BBC had suggested. It was a long, low note sounded at regular intervals of about thirty seconds, warning passing ships of the dangers of coming too close to the coastline. Of course, she realised too late that it was to the lighthouse that everyone was heading.

She had assumed that like Portland Bill, there would be a tea room and a museum to occupy the visitors and was disappointed to see that there was neither, just a lonely ice-cream van plying a very thin trade given the weather. There were however a couple of dozen cars each with a set of occupants sitting and watching the view, although the word 'view' was questionable given the thickness of the sea mist that was rolling in.

Rounding the corner she saw the lighthouse, sitting snugly against the rock below her on the coastline. Tucked away, the light was turning too, not at the same interval as the fog horn though, creating discordance between eye and ear.

The building was short and squat and surrounded by a high white wall with 'keep out' signs plastered on all the gates and entrances. Unlike Portland Bill which she thought of as tall and elegant, graceful against the weather and the English Channel. She supposed that on a clear day, there would be much to see, but at that moment, there was simply the thick mist, a beam from a lighthouse and the cliffs.

Rosemary could hear the beat of the waves against the base of the rocks and working her way cautiously to the edge she looked over and saw that the beach was perhaps a hundred feet down, too far to fall and survive. She moved back from the edge and carried on along the lane, which seemed to peter out into a track after the lighthouse. She could see quite clearly that the track culminated in a parking place that held even more cars, and beyond that there was a path that led steeply down from the cliff top to the beach below.

Realising that once again she was in the wrong shoes for scrambling, she turned around and headed to the nearest rock where she could park herself and rest before beginning the journey back home. The map in the cottage had suggested that she would be able to walk a circular route, but it meant following the path that led to the beach for at least a short way, and she was unsure what the footing would be like underneath and having no plans to end her life just as she was beginning to discover it, she decided that walking back along the lane was the most sensible course of action.

Although she could feel droplets hitting her face, it wasn't actually raining, it was simply the mist solidifying as it hit her skin. She relished the thought of being exposed to the elements in this way and it felt good to be inside the belly of Mother Nature at her most raw.

She listened to the sounds around her. Strangely the cars made little impact on her hearing and the people, if they were talking, could not be heard either. She was captivated by the music of the moment; the drip of water off the greenery, together with the call of the fog horn was entrancing. It spoke of a deeper level of understanding, knowledge of the sea and the land and the power that both had to change lives forever should the unwary make a mistake.

She felt an urge to be back and settled in her bolt hole, amongst the things she had brought with her. She also realised she'd only had cereal and two cups of tea which were beginning to make their presence known in her bladder. Reluctantly, she started back up the hill but still feeling the lightness of spirit that had so captivated her on the way down. She felt as if she were metamorphosing before her very own eyes, but she had no idea yet as to what the fate would be of the butterfly that she was beginning to hope would emerge.

It took longer to walk back to the cottage, probably because she hadn't realised quite how steep the road was. She was unfit and this was testing her poorly exercised body to its limits. Legs were objecting strongly and so were her back and hips. Old pains surfaced yet where once she would have complained, now she merely accepted that this was one more sign that she needed to do something about it all. By the end of the week she would, if nothing else be a little fitter if she walked every day like this.

She reached the crossroads and entered her lane. Pulling out the plastic bag reserved for the occasion, she started to pick the blackberries that were easily available.   Marvelling at how instinctively her fingers knew just how much pressure to use to detach the ripe fruit from its lock, she worked her way along the lane, picking just one or two here and there and not even from every bush, that way, there would be enough to go round for everyone.

By the time she had a bag full, she was yards from the cottage and happily she let herself into the house. After taking off shoes and coat and before drying off, she wandered into the kitchen with her bounty, tipping it into a bowl retrieved from the cupboard and filled it with water. Carefully she removed any husks or damaged parts from the succulent fruit, swirling them in water to remove any grit or sand they may have harboured. She finished the cleaning and then drained them and popped them into a plastic food bag for later. She would cook them with apple and honey and have them as a delicious dessert treat that night.

Sorting herself out upstairs she stripped off her damp jeans and tee-shirt and pulled on a pair of loose yoga pants and a long sleeved top. A pair of warm woolly socks completed the ensemble and she was back downstairs. It was well past noon and her stomach was creating its own musical accompaniment to the weather. Grabbing an apple and a pear, she made a cup of tea and settled down on the sofa just watching the light play against the chimney of the stove. She toyed with the idea of lighting it and once again dismissed it as it would get too hot. Instead she pulled the blanket over her and settled back on the sofa and closed her eyes.

Although she didn't sleep she did rest and when she opened her eyes some time later she noticed that the greyness had lifted somewhat from outside, it wasn't quite as all encompassing as it had been and there was the faintest hint of blue appearing in the cloud.

Moved to work, she gathered her laptop and switched it on; while she waited for it to get itself started she made another drink and set it down beside the sofa. Gathering the blanket and a large book from the bookcase, she placed the laptop on the book and both of them on her lap on top of the blanket, this was the first time she had ever tried to work at anything other than a desk and she was intrigued by how feasible it might be.

'Well this is a laptop and it is designed for laps, so it should work' she said out loud.

She worked steadily for the next few hours, pausing only to make fresh mugs of tea and to eat an apple or pear. By the time she stopped she had completed the reviews of all the reports she had brought with her, made copious notes for Jan, her assistant and was ready to start on the folders. She had also written a number of draft emails that would need to be sent once she had the opportunity to access her email accounts the following day. Satisfied with the progress she had made she felt that she deserved to stop for the remainder of the day as the light was thinning now and it was clear that the evening was rushing in to colour in the end of the day.

She turned the laptop off, moved it back to the dining table and once more made a simple supper of fish, salad and rice, this time finishing it off with yoghurt. Picking up her novel, she once again entered a different, alien world and rested in the arms of the author until she felt sleep overcome her and retired to bed. Just before she fell into sleep she remembered the blackberries, succulent and juicy in the fridge. A treat for later instead and she was content.

Chapter 6
Monday

Monday dawned dull and with thick black clouds spreading in from the West. There must have been a high wind in the jet stream because they rolled fast over the moorland and fields, every cloud becoming darker and angrier than its predecessor. The light which had streamed into the bedroom during previous mornings of her stay was dark and suggested it was earlier than it actually was, encouraging her to linger in the soft comfortableness of the bed for longer than she might otherwise have done. When she eventually decided to get up and make tea, she was surprised that it was already 11 o'clock and instead of taking her cup back to bed, placed it neatly on the side for drinking while she was dressing.

The water tickled her feet as the first drops traced their way over the shower base and she wriggled her toes both liking and disliking the sensation at the same time. The water splashed across her and as she washed she contemplated the day ahead.

Already she was settling into a routine that was comfortable. Without the need for an alarm clock her body was adopting a rhythm it was satisfied with and she wasn't inclined to upset it in any way. The world hadn't ended just because she had got up late; in fact it seemed a far more gracious host than she had first anticipated and didn't admonish her tardiness.

She was used to holidays that were as regimented as much if not more, than her home life. Sightseeing was compulsory for, according to James, there was no point in visiting somewhere if you didn't pack as much as possible in. A brief image of the '29 countries in 16 days' tour that was an urban myth the British perpetuated about Americans, 'ah yes, if it's day 13 this should be Rome' came quickly to mind.

Smiling at the thought and wondering if it were actually true, the fact that she could even consider the truth of it was probably because her own experiences were not too dissimilar. James had been eager to make sure that they got their money's worth out of every holiday, insisting that they did every trip, every monument, every stately home or garden that they could possibly fit in during the week, occasionally two, they took as their 'annual holiday'. Not for James the indolence of lying in bed or a gentle walk into the village with a snooze on the sofa, oh no, that would be sacrilege and an abuse of the opportunity they had, 'an opportunity', he was fond of telling her, 'that many don't have and you ought to be grateful'.

There were many words one could associate with James and 'ought' was a contender for the top position. Others included, 'should' and 'no' and 'don't' along with phrases like 'we can't afford it' and 'that's too expensive' and the one she hated the most 'think of others, you are so selfish'. She tried to be charitable and remember words of encouragement and support but was hard pressed to recall times when this had happened. In the end she gave up and simply dried herself instead.

Downstairs she decided to miss breakfast; it was almost midday and seemed a little foolish to start it now. She plucked an apple and a pear from the fruit bowl and took her tea into the sitting room. Glancing out of the window she realised that if she wanted to walk, she would need to do it sooner rather than later as the clouds were becoming heavier and darker by the minute.

Putting on her trainers, she decided to walk down to the village shop for some lemon juice, that would be just the thing to add to tea instead of milk for a change and it gave her a good excuse to go and have a longer look around. Popping money in her pocket and looping the key around her neck she pulled the door too behind her. Looking skywards she realised that it might be wise to take a coat and perhaps an umbrella too so unlocked the door and grabbed both from off the hooks nearby.

She wasn't far along the lane when the rain started and she put her coat on and the umbrella up. The air was still warm and the rain when it touched her skin was too. She decided to carry on with her walk, it might be like this all day and she didn't want to miss out on what was fast becoming an important part of her new routine. She walked swiftly avoiding the puddles that were forming and by the time she had reached the main road it was coming down hard, so hard that her jeans were starting to get wet at the front. The further she walked the harder the rain fell and it looked like it was going to be set for the day. By the time she reached the shop, her whole front was wet through and her trainers were starting to let water in. But she was exhilarated, she was having fun.

The rain was not going to let go its grip of the landscape easily and it was coming straight down abusing one of the notion that the high winds above the clouds were having any impact at all. This was a rain belt that was definitely not going to move anytime soon.

After making her purchase and stuffing it into her pocket, she stepped out into the onslaught again and became aware very quickly that there was a slight pitch to the rain for this time it was the back of her legs that were getting wet, very quickly indeed.

Before very long she was soaked through from the bottom of her jacket which lay above her waist right down to her socks. She relished the feel of the heavy wet cotton against her legs, its weight serving to prove that she was real and a part of the landscape through which she was walking. Bound to the earth and nature, she was as integral a piece in this jigsaw of life as the slug she spied on the road or the scents she smelt as the rain encouraged flowers to share their secrets.

The rain was so intense, that by the time she reached the lane, her trainers which had been merely wet through, were actually starting to fill with water. She could feel the slop, slop, slop through her socks and whilst it wasn't exactly unpleasant she was aware that if she walked too long like this then she might end up with blisters.

Grateful that she didn't have too far to go, she turned a corner and realised too late that the lane was rapidly turning into stream, and quite a deep stream at that.

Two choices presented themselves, she could walk back and along the road or she could carry on, she chose the latter, she was wet anyway and couldn't possibly get any wetter so she strode confidently into the water that lapped across the road, allowing it to flow into and over her shoes. It gave her a great deal of satisfaction to know that she would never have done anything so bold or reckless at home, the threat of the disapproval she might face for potentially ruining a perfectly good pair of shoes would have made her stay at home, only going out when the rain had died and she'd be able to get to the car easily.

She stripped off in the vestibule not caring that anyone might see her take her trainers, socks, jeans and knickers off. She was far too wet and far too polite to want to drip all the way to the kitchen. Strolling through the sitting room she was very conscious of the open curtains and the lack of privacy but made no move to close them and protect herself, if anyone were out in this then they probably deserved the scintillating vision of looking at her aging body she thought.

In the kitchen the clothes were deposited in the washing machine and it was turned on to 'spin' and she turned her attention to her trainers. It was too wet to put them outside so stuffing them with the newspaper she had brought but not deigned to read was her only option really. Everything dealt with she could finally sort herself out.

Upstairs she rubbed her lower body hard with her still damp towel. She was no longer really wet, but her skin had a coldness to it from her exposure to the elements and she thought it prudent to warm it through. Pulling on pink PJ's she decided that the rest of the day would be spent holed up in the cottage with her book and her work.

Opening the top half of the stable door, she let the sound of the heavy rain enter the cottage. Protected by the overhang, nothing was able to enter the little room and she was reluctant to let go of her experience just yet, wishing to keep it going for as long as possible.

The rain continued unabated, bouncing from the sky onto the ground, the shrubs and the gutter and it was the last that pleased her the most because it afforded the loudest sounds as the droplets hit metal shattering into a thousand more before coming to rest on the gravel in the garden.

Stretching out supine on the sofa she reached for her novel and allowed herself to lose all sense of time in the words and pages she was reading.

A holiday, she realised was for drawing all the scattered pieces of yourself back together and giving them time to meld and become a whole human being again. They were not the time to make things even worse by cramming in every sight and sound on a packed tourist schedule.

She was cosy, she was comfortable and once again she fell asleep.

Waking sometime later was a painful process; somehow she had become wedged on the sofa with her neck in an odd position curled into her shoulder. Untangling her limbs she stretched out the tension and was aware that the rain was still drumming as fiercely as it had been when she had first laid down. Content that all was right with the world, she lay back and pondered on her current position. Here she was sitting all alone on a sofa in a cottage as close to the edge of the world as she could get and she was happy, for the first time in many years she truly realised she was happy. Happiness was not, it seemed, great bouts of laughter all the time, it was a quiet contentment and feeling that she had the right to be where she was, doing what she was doing for the reason she was doing it.

If James had his way she would never have come, never experienced this great sense of peace with herself. He was against such endeavours of the self, although he encouraged personal development in the form of such suitable pursuits as evening classes in languages, literature and crafts.

Gathering herself up, she moved into the kitchen counting the number of steps as she went, five. She decided to measure the space she was in and placed her back against the oven and then strode off across the kitchen and through the sitting room to the base of the stairs, ten paces, and then from underneath the open stair case to the front window, eight paces. It wasn't even as big as her bedroom at home and yet she felt more complete in this tiny space than she did anywhere else in the world.

It contained everything she needed and nothing more, wondering idly what it might be like to live in the cottage she thought about her possessions at home and considered how they might fit into the space available. As she did so, she realised that there was little she actually saw belonging in a place like this. Her books, of course, her music system, clothes and a few odd ornaments given to her by friends and relatives over the years, it was shocking how little she realised she had considered necessary or important and in that moment a revelation occurred to her,

Perhaps I don't need it.

The thought was so rapid in its forming and was so definite, almost as if it had been waiting for her to make the mental leap in order for it to take centre stage that she knew it came from the heart, from the depths of her soul and body and with that realisation came something even more challenging, perhaps she didn't need anything!

The challenge she had just presented herself seemed so great that she needed to ground it. Her mind was playing games with her, games she wasn't prepared for and could hardly comprehend.

'Tea', she thought, that would help to settle her disquiet about where this week was taking her.

Her hands were shaking as she filled the kettle with water; all her life she had craved excitement, expecting that it would be delivered in the form of a hectic social life or a cultural overload and here it was presenting itself to her in a tiny cottage in an unpretentious village in Cornwall.

There were no bright lights and fanfares to herald its coming, just a slow dawning of the relevancy of her life and its place in the world.

The excitement came from knowing that she had the power within her to change her life if she wanted to. She was gripped with a powerful urge to strip off and run outside naked, just test the waters, but refrained from doing so, not because she couldn't do it but more from the recognition that she didn't want to be arrested, at least not just yet.

The kettle pinged off and she filled her cup with boiling water, soaking the tea bag that lay within which gave up its flavour and scent willingly, sacrificing itself on the altar of her need. She returned to her post on the sofa and thought about the many little things that had occurred in just a few short days, little things that of themselves didn't mean much but taken as a whole were hugely transformative.

Freedom beckoned and she was bound to follow.

Not wanting to upset the delicate internal work which was obviously taking place in her mind by over analysing it, she decided to carry on with the work she had brought with her. It would be a great distraction and she imagined how good she would feel once she had got all the outstanding reports and administrative tasks that had built up over the last few months out of the way.

She got up and gathered folders, pens, paper and laptop, placing them all on the far end of the sofa from the bit she had claimed as her own. She was in two minds about her mobile phone too; it would give her Internet access if she wanted it, but did she really want to be connected to the outside world just yet!

At that moment it announced a new message had arrived, once again its timing seemed impeccable and she flicked it on and read the words the message contained.

'Glad you're Ok, I'm here if you want to talk. X'.

Smiling at the correct use of grammar, she noted the perfect spelling and complete sentences was a pleasure she encountered infrequently, most people these days seemed happy to txt spk. Tapping quickly she sent back a reply.

'Thanks, appreciate it. X'

She hoped the X at the end would convey enough emotion to be understood for what it meant. It was a 'don't call me, I'll call you' message, her burgeoning self confidence was still too new and too fragile to be subjected to any degree of scrutiny by a third party and besides, she was relishing her self imposed exile, knowing that if anyone else were allowed in, even by telephone, that somehow the magic might fragment and disappear, trapping her in a half life from which there might be no escape.

Turning the phone off was the best way to discourage any further contact should there be any and realising that her laptop had a clock too meant that there was no need to keep it available every minute of the day. Long ago, men and women had lived their whole lives by the rising and setting of the sun and moon and had tracked the movement of the years by the turning of the stars and her body was adjusting, slowly, to a new rhythm of life that was more in sync with these natural time pieces so she decided to go with the flow.

Retuning to her laptop she switched it on, took a deep swallow of tea from the waiting mug and opened up the first document. Methodically working her way through the folder by her side, she was meticulous in the completion of the forms and it was with a great sense of satisfaction that everything balanced, first time.

I really must do this more often, she thought.

Recalling that more often than not her tension and the constant interruptions from colleagues and staff meant that she would often spend twice as long on the same task and it would still be wrong.

Rosemary loved her job and had, as a result of the personnel development programme and Institute of Personnel Management qualifications she had taken, risen quite quickly for a council to the dizzy heights of Senior Personnel Manager.

She was well thought of by the small team that reported to her, acknowledged for being firm, but fair and was one of the few senior management team members who believed in praising good work. As a result her team out-performed almost all others when it came to the increasing number of Government targets that were supposed to be met, her team wanted to please her because they knew that they would be rewarded with something, even if it was as small as a 'thank you', but more often than not, with some form of personal development or task they could really get their teeth into.

Over the years there had been a chance to expand her role further still and with changes to things like The Data Protection Act, there had been an opportunity for someone to take responsibility for ensuring compliance in every part of the organisation. Rosemary had taken to it like a duck to water, realising that she loved consulting even more and had started helping local businesses with their compliance issues.

Increasing pressure by successive Governments and reductions in funding meant it became more and more important to try to draw in additional funds from somewhere and a new department was created that had her at its heart.

By providing support to local businesses it was able to draw on the vast pool of local consultants that offered help in an enormous number of areas, in short she had found herself just about running her own business, reporting to no-one but the Chief Executive and the Leader of the Council.

The three of them held regular meetings, often over sumptuous lunches at a local hotel, plotting and planning how to help the businesses of the town still further. She became adept at applying for grant funding from an enormous variety of sources and this allowed her team to expand to include full time fundraising professionals, as well as the administrative staff. Between them, they pulled in an extra ten percent of the Council's earnings; money which went directly to building the local economy in ways that it wouldn't have been possible to do otherwise.

As she worked through her folders and documents Rosemary realised that even this could change, in fact anything was possible, anything at all.

Chapter 7

They had married the following year, almost twelve months after they had first met and in front of two hundred and fifty guests, a motley crew comprising family, lots of family, friends and hangers on, they had made their vows and at the time of saying them had been earnest in meaning each and every word. It was only later, as the years passed by that they would come to realise just how much a sacrifice they would both have to make to hopes and dreams before things turned full circle and they were alone once more.

It would have been apt to say that the day had been dull, grey or even wet given the future they were yet to be presented with; but in fact it was beautiful, one of those rare days in September that was warm and humid and that had all the promise of an Indian Summer to come.

The bride was radiant in a white, off the shoulder dress and with three small bridesmaids in tow she glided down the aisle to her beau full of love and longing. He was handsome in his morning suit, with peach cravat and a buttonhole which matched her bouquet. Tall and with an athletic build, it was easy to overlook the weak chin and the small mouth.

On that day though they were both anticipating their future and hoping that in the other would be provided the other half of themselves that they had found lacking.

Despite assurances to their parents to the contrary, they had in fact tested out their love making skills already. They were both virgins and with the naivety of the same had assumed that with time and practice that they would both get better at it. Their early fumbling never really amounted to much and she more often that not had found herself frustrated by his inability to make even a pretence at satisfying her. In fact, he didn't know he should, his sex education had mostly consisted of talk amongst the boys at school and then later on porn channels and men's magazines, all of which suggested that a man simply had to enter a woman for her to have the most amazing orgasm. As a result, he assumed that she was frigid.

They found relief in a wedding present from his friends which had been delivered on his stag night. The package contained one copy of 'The Perfumed Garden', one copy of 'The Karma Sutra' and one copy of 'The Joy of Sex'.

His friends never really knew just how much that gift contributed to the longevity of their marriage nor just how inexperienced James was, for despite his age and his looks, he had been shy of women, warned off them by his mother who had foreseen her son being taken advantage of by some tart who would get pregnant and force him into an unsuitable marriage.

Rosemary on the other hand was a past master at heavy petting, but had always shied away from going the whole way because of a feeling that she only wanted to give herself to the man she would marry. Whether this was misguided or not was anybody's guess but without the unexpected stag night gift there was every chance that their marriage might not have lasted more than a couple of years.

Their shining faces and loving gestures on the day of their wedding hid their impatience for the proceedings to be over. They had agreed to a large wedding because both sets of parents had wished it and had paid for the whole affair. They wanted it to be over because they had yet to try out the present that had been given them and they were eager to see what would happen when they were alone in the honeymoon suite of the hotel their reception was taking place in.

Eventually the day drew to a close with the DJ announcing the departure of the newly married Mr and Mrs James Edwards. The crowd of guests clapped as they made their way sedately through the double doors at the end of the banqueting suite and then they fled, clutching each other's hand to their room, laughing and giggling like school children.

The wedding night was long and seemed to go on forever. While Rosemary ran a bath for them both to sink into, James read out passages from the books and showed her the pictures. There were some they were instinctively drawn to and others that both felt would never be acceptable although they kept these thoughts to themselves for fear of upsetting the other. That was the night that James learnt about his role in his wife's pleasure, realising that it was not a reflex action that caused an orgasm and his opinion of her changed, no longer was she frigid; she became a sexy siren that just had to look at him and he was turned on.

For her part, Rosemary relished the domination she achieved over James when they were making love and used it to full effect. Their honeymoon was another success and they both returned triumphant, their marriage had been consummated and they could now look forward to happy ever after, because that was what happened in all the great fairy stories wasn't it?

Before they had married, Rosemary had been very careful to explain to James that she didn't want children. She explained her reasoning and had said that it was important he know because she didn't want him to resent her later on. He had agreed wholeheartedly and had even held her hand, looking into her eyes and saying that it was fine, he was happy with what made her happy; all the while privately knowing that this was not going to go down well with his mother, who desperately wanted to be a grandmother along with all her friends. He assumed she would change her mind after they were married because all women get broody don't they, biological clock and all that and imagined that they would have just one, a girl probably, who would look just the same as the photograph his mother kept of herself aged 6, all rosebud lips and ringlets.

The first year of marriage passed quickly. They moved to Birmingham and Rosemary quickly found a new job in the local authority, it was so close to where they were living that she could even walk to work if she wanted, but she preferred to take the bus with James, sharing a tender kiss goodbye when she got off at her stop, she often waved to him as the bus pulled away and he would sometimes wave back, depending on who was looking of course.

Pooling their savings they were able to put a largish deposit down on a three bedroom house with a good sized garden and a garage. The mortgage was tight but with both of them working they were managing just fine. They presented the very aura of young married respectability.

It was the following September when his mother first mentioned grandchildren to her new daughter-in-law. It was a subtle move, one that might have barely registered if Rosemary hadn't already told James she didn't want children.

'That small bedroom of yours would look lovely in pink!'

Rosemary wasn't sure how to react, being a wife and a daughter-in-law were still new to her and she was only just 21 and unversed in the ways of adult behaviour. She murmured something non-committal and took her leave.

When James came home from the office after another late night, she explained what had happened and wondered out loud what she might say that would let his mother know it was never going to happen. James had forgotten the conversation before their wedding and hung on to the belief that they would one day have a little girl with rosebud lips and ringlets who would be called Lucy after his mother.

They had their first major row. It was short and bloody and each retreated to a different part of the house to lick their wounds. They had both said some dreadful things to the other and in the process had begun to notice that there were some potential areas for conflict that had still been unexplored. Once again though, both kept these feelings private, focusing instead on the hurts inflicted that were directly relevant to the current point of contention, children.

He had accused her of being selfish; she had reminded him that she had made it quite clear that children were not on the agenda of her life. He said that was the only reason he had bought a house with three bedrooms, a garden and a garage, she retorted that she hadn't wanted it in the first place and would have been happy with a flat in the City Centre with the art galleries, museums and theatres.

He repeated that he worked his fingers to the bone to provide for them both and this was all the thanks he got and she replied that she worked too and it would be quite nice to see her husband in the evening sometimes instead of spending most of them alone.

And so it went on, the list of hurts being dredged up and hung out to dry was legion; they were both shocked by the ferocity of their attacks and resolved, privately not to do it again.

What didn't happen though was a resolution to the question in hand and instead an uneasy truce was drawn an unspoken agreement that no more would be said about the matter.

In the future whenever any of the parents mentioned the word 'grandchildren', they were left with the impression that this was an on-going quest of the young couple who were unfortunate enough not to have been successful just yet.

Despite the argument life in the Edwards household continued, she was working towards her qualifications and he had finally been offered a junior partnership with his firm. His monthly trips to Edinburgh became weekly trips and he widened his area of responsibility to include part of the Southern regions too.

Their life settled into a comfortable rut; his mother came for supper on Wednesdays and Fridays, and she would return the favour by cooking Sunday lunch for which they had to present themselves at one o'clock precisely.

In between times, the house became a project and they improved every area of it, building a conservatory at the back, replacing the kitchen and bathroom, landscaping the garden and turning the contentious small bedroom into an office they both shared, she for her studying and he for the work he brought home in the evenings he was in Birmingham.

Their lives were increasingly separate, but every Friday evening, after his mother had been taken home, they retired to bed early and they had sex, it became fixed in stone. Sex on Fridays, never in the mornings, or on Sundays, it was always on Fridays and followed exactly the same routine every time and included an orgasm for her and one for him. Neither seemed to realise that there might be anything wrong with this arrangement, both assuming that this was how all marriages were.

The subject of children was never mentioned again for fear of causing another argument and it was only years later that both were able to reflect that perhaps this had not been a 'good thing' for it lay like a gulf between them which they were never able to cross and the gulf just got wider and wider and neither of them really noticed it happening.

Chapter 8

The folder she was working on was complete, the reports written the forms totalled and the expenses all signed off. It was late now and there was a lull in the rain outside, in fact it seemed to be brightening up just a little.

Making yet another cup of tea, Rosemary contemplated another walk to stretch out legs too long still from sitting and decided that as soon as the rain stopped completely she would go out for more blackberries. Remembering the ones already in the fridge, she transferred them to the freezer figuring that they would lose less Vitamin C if they were frozen, at least that's what all the frozen food adverts kept telling her.

Having completed what she had set out to do and unwilling to sit down again, she was restless and moved about the house clutching her mug between her hands. She stopped every now and then to look at a picture or pick up a book, but nothing absorbed her and she realised she was itching to be out once more, rain or no rain.

Draining the last of the drink, she reached for her trainers, but they were still completely sodden from the morning, a quick glance outside showed it was still drizzling so summer shoes would be no good, therefore boots it had to be.

Pink PJs were even less appropriate and it was necessary to make a change of clothing, her jeans were still soaking so she reached for a favourite pair of leggings and a long jumper.

If they get wet, they get wet, she thought.

Downstairs she zipped on boots and cautiously zipped up the too small jacket, it was damp but not wet so it would do. The rain had stopped by the time she stepped outside and she walked briskly along the lane to where the blackberry bushes started and began picking, just the odd one here and there again, never taking more that two or three from a stem and often just one from a bush. Her fingers worked instinctively, checking each one for firmness before the sharp tug that released it from its bud. A few were over-ripe and they burst all over her fingers, staining them a dark purple in the process.

She had been working her way along the road for about ten minutes when a voice called out 'hello'.

Unsure whether it was referring to her she looked up and around and saw a large, friendly looking woman approaching with a chocolate Labrador on a leash. She was sensibly dressed in a long waterproof waxed coat and a big hat.

The woman passed her by with a cheery 'hope you get enough for a blackberry and apple pie' and was gone, dragged along by the dog.

Rosemary smiled and called out after her 'oh I think so' and returned to her work.

She carried on all along the lane, just picking from the left hand side of the road this time, she didn't want to deplete the bushes for other pickers and the birds. She turned around and walked slowly back up the lane and rounding the last bend, she encountered the chocolate Labrador and the woman again who this time stopped in the road and smiled broadly.

Indicating the bag of blackberries she suggested that Rosemary might have picked them all before she could get a chance, and entering into the spirit of the conversation, Rosemary confirmed that she thought she had left plenty for others to come along.

'You're not from round here are you?' are you the woman enquired.

Rosemary's reply was short and succinct 'no, I've rented a cottage'.

'Ah, on holiday'.

'Yes, you could say that'.

'Mmmm how long are you here for?'

'Just until Friday'.

'Oh good, come along to the coffee morning on Wednesday in the village hall and we can have a chat, starts ten am. My name's Liz by the way, what's yours?'

'Rosemary and thank you, I will'.

They smiled at each other and with the conversation over Liz moved away swiftly to be swallowed up by the corner Rosemary had just come around.

She continued back to the cottage thinking about the encounter she had just had with Liz. What an extraordinary woman, she was obviously used to getting her own way though because the invitation had been issued more like an order rather than a suggestion that it might be something worth doing.

Putting it to the back of her mind Rosemary thought it might be fun to go along and see what happens, perhaps Liz might be able to tell her something about the young woman that lived next door.

Without her even realising it, the day had morphed into evening and the light was fading fast. She drew the curtains on both sides of the cottage and in all rooms and made her supper. This time she treated herself to the nettle soup she had bought at the farmers market on Saturday and its hot creaminess warmed her body throughout. It didn't take long to eat and the rest of the evening stretched before her. But there was no hint of boredom, there was no pressure to do anything and she found herself stretching out once more on the sofa, this time facing the TV so that she could watch the flickering screen before her.

Once more she channel hopped until she found a documentary about life in a British inner city, more than once it made her cry, not the long hot tears of the day before, but shorter fresher tears in acknowledgement of something that touched her deep inside and recognising that her life had, by all accounts, been privileged.

Despite their problems and issues, James was not a bad man, he wasn't cruel and he'd never hurt her, physically anyway. He was more a product of his generation, and his mother she thought ruefully. It hadn't been his fault that they had drifted apart over the years, she was equally responsible for the distance they had created; but whereas she had tried to do something about it, even suggesting that they go to marriage counselling, he had stuck his head in the sand and refused to acknowledge there was a problem that needed addressing.

She sighed; the guilt she felt at her abandonment of him was intense, even now twelve months later. Despite everything that had happened, she felt responsible for the final outcome and that would never diminish. Instead, she had to find a way to live with it so that she would be able to carry on.

The programme she had been watching finished and she made her way to the kitchen for a cup of camomile tea. In bed, she sat, thoughtful about all that had happened over the last 12 months and knew that this was exactly where she needed to be right now. No amount of feeling guilty was going to neither make it better nor make it right and she couldn't turn the clock back.

She had started a process of transformation and it had to be played out to the end, because it had to be worth it, all the heartache, the internal accusations and the watchful eyes of her soul.

The dreams started almost as soon as she had closed her eyes. In the first she was drowning and there were faces all around her reaching out to her, but instead of helping her, they were pushing her back under the water, not letting her surface to catch her breath. As she struggled she became hotter and the water evaporated from her skin and became fire and the fire raged without heat but with an intensity of light that she had never thought possible. She was being cleansed from within, cleansed by dying, by drowning and by fire.

The scene changed again, this time she was back in Edinburgh and was running from the station but instead of crashing into James she avoided him and carried on running, running past him. Over the bridge and onto Princes Street and he was just watching her run and run without stopping her or shouting out.

As she ran she became aware of people shouting and screams, slowly she realised the screams were hers, and the people shouting were the same people who had tried to keep her under the water. She recognised faces, Lucy, James mother; her mother and father, a neighbour or two and people from work and then Adam.

Her eyes settled on his, why was he shouting at her and trying to drown her?

All the time she was screaming and struggling and drowning and the water became fire and the fire became water until suddenly all was still and she was sat, a small child once more, in her mothers bedroom watching her mother combing out her hair whilst her mother was talking to her, telling her that she could be anything she wanted to be and that she never wanted her to have the life that she'd had. But that she needed to reach for the stars if she wanted to have them, because they wouldn't come down to earth to get her and that wishing it wouldn't make it happen she had to do things and reach for the things she wanted.

Insights came thick and fast, she finally understood how James had expected her to fulfil the parts of himself he could never express and how she had done the same to him. Each wanting the other to complete themselves and make themselves whole, without realising they already held the power to do that within their own hearts, if only they had trusted enough to trust that the universe wanted what was best for them. Their lesson had been to stay true to the potential they had been born with and they had forsaken that by ignoring it.

The dreams continued, the scenes flashing by so quickly sometimes that they barely had time to register. She saw horses and cowboys and dreamt of gunfights at the OK Corral.

Her brain was whirling her through a vast number of images each fighting for space to become real enough to be understood before fading into the background as another took its place. Carpets and houses, rings and bouquets of flowers and a child with rosebud lips and ringlets, they were all there for her to see. Some she understood, others had no known meaning, but clearly were from her deep subconscious, that part of her that was hidden even from her own mind.

She struggled to hang on to them all, knowing that she needed to remember what was playing out before her, but recognising that already she was forgetting bits that had just past. Sadly, she allowed them to go and stopped trying so hard and in the letting go they stopped and she settled back into a deep restorative sleep. Her brain had done its best; the rest would be up to her strength of character and will now.

Chapter 9
Tuesday

When she woke, it was with a start. The bed clothes were tangled around her and the sheet had come loose from its moorings in the night, clearly it had been a rough one. She remembered that she had been dreaming and that there were important things she had been told, but she couldn't for the life of her remember what they were.

The feeling of loss was intense, like being given a valuable diamond and then losing it somewhere but knowing that it was hidden in the open and if she could only open her eyes wide enough she would spot it in the corner.

Saddened, she got out of bed and made her way downstairs to make tea. As she drew the curtains back, she noticed that the gerberas and sweet peas had started to shed their petals overnight, she fancied it was nature's way of reflecting her mood and gathered the fallen colours into her hand to put them in the bin.

Despite the sun shining outside the window, she felt listless and grey. It had not been a good night and she didn't feel as well rested as she might have done. Perhaps this was the day for a swim.

There were no clouds in the sky and the sun felt hot through the glass. A swim might just be the trick she needed to get herself back to the land of possibilities she had entered the evening before.

Without pausing for breakfast she dressed quickly, figuring she would shower when she got back as there was no point in wasting water. She put clothes on over her swimming costume and grabbed the pink beach towel she had brought for the purpose and then added her walking shoes.

Having already experienced the slippery nature of the path to the beach, she had no intention of breaking an ankle on the way down.

It took about 20 minutes to get to the head of the cove and she was careful to make her way down the path that was clearly marked, rather than taking the more direct route. The sun was warm on her back and by the time she had scrambled over the last of the rocks she was panting and hot.

There was no one else around which was just as she wanted and she slipped out of her outer clothes quickly. Leaving them in a pile she made her way slowly over the sand, avoiding the occasional sharp rock that threatened unwary toes and feet. The water looked cool and inviting and was an intense shade of blue, reflecting the sky above beautifully.

This would make a fabulous painting, she thought, once again regretting that she didn't have an artist's bone in her body.

The light was perfect and she began to get an inkling of an understanding about why the northern coasts of Cornwall were a haven for artists. There was also something about the light of a September morning too; it was softer somehow and gentler than those of high summer, a hint perhaps of the lengthening of the nights and shortening of the days, the colours were more muted and shading more subtle, she had the faintest feeling of being in a Monet painting.

Dipping one toe in the water, she realised it wasn't as cold as she had feared. The beach shelved slowly and the sand was warm underfoot already. She walked bravely into the sea and once she was up to thigh height allowed herself to sink down under the water to her shoulders. She experienced a slight tingle throughout her body as the cool water moved up the exposed parts of her skin but it was refreshing and she knew that she'd get used to the cold very quickly.

Breathing deeply she struck out from the shoreline practising a few quick strokes she swam confidently into deeper water. She was a strong swimmer and had no fear of water, allowing the waves to wash her where they would and keeping a wary eye on the beach making sure she wasn't drifting too far out.

The wave when it came was unexpected and fierce. She hadn't been anticipating it and was momentarily knocked off her balance and thrown underwater, gasping and struggling she reached for the surface again. Her head clear of the water, she was panting from the exertion and at being taken by surprise.

As she trod water she became aware of a strong current beneath and struck out for the beach, but the current held her where she was and she found she was barely moving in the direction she wanted to go.

Panic started to creep into her and she swam harder, but the harder she swam the stronger the current seemed and the firmer it held her in its grasp. Too late, she realised how stupid she had been to swim alone with no one to see her or help her if she needed it.

Her panic mounting she tried harder and harder and with every stroke she took she maintained almost the same position. Her efforts took her minutely towards her goal but her strength was fading. Unfit, she hadn't seriously swum for years and it was showing. Her muscles were aching and her lungs were fit to burst and she felt she wouldn't have the strength to make it back.

In that moment she remembered a part of her dream the night before and the drowning and thought she understood. This was retribution for what she had done, it was what she deserved. Images flashed before her eyes.

So this is what they mean about seeing your whole life just before death.

A rainbow of memories cascaded into her brain, each bigger and brighter than the last, all piling on top of each other, mingling and merging and painting the landscape of her life, until she couldn't tell where one started and another one ended.

And, in the moment of her giving up and giving in, another enormous wave came beneath her and carried her into the shallower waters of the beach, dumping her unceremoniously with a thump on the sand beneath.

Laughing hysterically she was aware of what a lucky escape she had just had and imagined her body being found washed up and bloated by immersion some miles along the coast, or perhaps being eaten by the sea life that encountered it. There were cold water sharks spotted off the coast every so often after all.

She climbed to her feet, bruised from her landing and limped back up the beach to her clothes. Pulling the towel around her she sat down again to recover her composure before attempting to get dressed. The sea looked so blue and so inviting and deceptively calm. There was barely a ripple on its surface.

And then she saw it.

A grey seal poked its head out of the water and looked straight at her, they looked at each other for what seemed like hours, but was probably just a few seconds and then it bobbed its head, as if in acknowledgement and flipped back under water and away.

She took it as a good omen.

She was feeling cold, shock was probably setting in, she needed something to warm her and calm her nerves. Drying herself thoroughly she re-dressed and headed back up the beach to the path she had latterly come down. Climbing gingerly over the rocks she reached the base and started the long walk back to the cottage.

Her legs were aching and her arms felt leaden, the energy she had when she went into the water had left her and on her walk back to the cottage she was exhausted and pale.

Barely noticing what was going on around her she didn't see or hear the car coming until it was almost upon her and with just enough time to allow her to jump into the hedgerow it stopped, pinning her to the wall. A window was lowered and a face peered out at her.

'Are you alright love? You look like you've seen a ghost.'

The face was kindly and the eyes were bright with a mop of striking white hair sitting over the top of the whole.

She felt like she was looking into the eyes of her grandfather and started to cry. Wracking sobs caught at her throat and she struggled to apologise for her state.

Without a word the car pulled away and she was forced to admit she had made a complete fool of herself.

Resuming her journey back up the road, she became aware of a second car coming along behind her and stepped into the side to allow it to pass. However, instead of passing it stopped again.

Bloody hell I must look like a right state, she thought and rubbed her eyes fiercely to remove any lingering tears.

It was the same car and the same friendly face looked out.

'Hop in love, you look all done in'.

Gratefully she climbed into the passenger seat, not bothering to even acknowledge the thought that said it might not be a good idea.

'Where are you staying?'

'I'm renting a cottage just at the end of North Lane' she explained.

'Ok, I'll drop you off at the end of the road'.

He smiled and didn't make any further enquiries into what the problem was, and she was content to just settle back into the seat and close her eyes for the few minutes it took them to arrive at her destination.

He touched her arm gently, 'we're here'.

He was nodding in the general direction of the cottage. 'Will you be alright now?'

'Thank you, I'll be fine and you've been so kind'.

She was so grateful for the small gift he'd given her that she was overcome once more with tears, but this time she was smiling through them.

'I will be just fine now'. She climbed out of the car and watched him as he turned around and headed back the way they had come.

There are angels on earth she thought and walked back towards her small cottage.

Once indoors she dumped her wet things in the washing machine, filling the powder drawer with washing tablets she'd brought with her and turning it on. She filled the kettle and went upstairs to climb into something warmer and comfortable. There was no doubt about it, she'd had a fright, one which she wouldn't want repeating.

She thought it was kind of that old gentleman to give me a lift what a shame I forgot to ask his name.

She made her way to the kitchen once more and made a mug of tea, this time liberally laced with honey as well as milk. Nestling on the sofa, she pulled the blanket around her and thought about her recent encounter with the sea. It could have gone so horribly wrong, she could be dead by now and she was ashamed of herself for being so stupid, perhaps James had been right all along, perhaps she was selfish, never thinking of anyone other than herself. The thought of a child or two perhaps finding her body was horrendous; it could have scarred them for life. For some unfathomable reason that thought cheered her, perhaps it was the image of them finding the beached whale of her body and she was laughing again, sure that she was this time, really going mad to be laughing in the face of something so serious.

Aware that her stomach was empty and that she needed food, she headed once more for the kitchen and filled a bowl with cereal adding a banana and yoghurt as well, she headed back to the sitting room and the dining table.

In the night a spider had made its last journey and she was presented with a tiny corpse hanging by an invisible thread. The synchronicity was not lost on her and she acknowledged the universes attempt to let her know that this could have been her fate today. Grateful for being the one still alive, she couldn't face eating with such a strong reminder hanging in front of her so she gathered it up into a tissue and deposited it into the kitchen bin. Returning to the dining table she resumed her breakfast and drank the tea she had made.

She ate slowly, reverentially, acknowledging her lucky escape in every delicious mouthful. The flavours of the food were more intense than she had ever noticed before, the smell of banana stronger. She could distinguish the lemon in the tea and the honey provided a sweet overtone of flavour, serving like salt, to bring out the rest of the flavours in her mouth. She realised that this was the way her body was reacting to its shock, she was grateful nevertheless and appreciated the meal all the more.

After she had finished and cleared the dishes away it became imperative that she occupy her mind with something other than thoughts of what might have been.

She lit the stove; even though it was warm outside, she was still chilled and knew that this was probably the fastest way she had of warming up. Pulling the blanket firmly around her, she watched the flames as they started to take hold of the paper and kindling, once they were blazing away she added the first of the logs from the basket. The warmth from the stove spread outwards across the tiny room slowly, starting with her feet which were closet to the source of heat and finally reaching her head. She was sleepy even though it was not yet midday and she allowed herself to stretch once more along the whole length of the sofa, drifting back into an inky blackness where there were, mercifully, no dreams to speak of.

Judging by the light coming through the window it was mid afternoon when she woke for the second time that day. Stretching out carefully she noticed that the fire had gone out in the stove, but that the room was warm and cosy. She settled back into the sofa once more, reluctant to move out from the security of the blanket and the comfort of the cushions and simply stared at the fireplace for a very long time.

Carefully sending her attention all over her body, she was relieved to note that there were no traces of shock left in her at all and that she was once more relaxed and loose. In fact she felt better than she had done when she first woke that morning which was a result, given everything that had already occurred in one half of a single day.

She still felt no desire to explore any further than she was already doing and a trip into St Ives or Penzance didn't appeal. Casting her mind over the work she had brought with her she wondered if there was something easy that would occupy the time and her hands whilst allowing her to rest mentally. Then she remembered the file of expense receipts. This was the one area she was particularly lax in and she was regularly rebuked for not putting in her expenses claims on time.

With diary to hand and the folder full of receipts, she began the long and boring, task of completing claim forms, thus affording herself a mental respite because she needed to pay enough attention to make sure there were no mistakes made, but not too much that it taxed her.

The job didn't take too long to complete at all, in fact she was done in less than two hours and was soon kicking her heels again wondering what to do. The work she had brought with her was becoming boring and the one interesting item left on her agenda was to prepare a presentation for her colleagues about a new area they were about to get involved in. She wasn't relishing the thought, she hated speaking in public even though everyone said she was good at it, but at least she knew the subject matter inside out. Thinking about the amount of work involved in creating the presentation she dismissed it for that day, putting it off until later in the week and decided instead to make a drink and sit out in the garden which was now possible because the garden bench had dried out after the rain of the day before.

Instead of her usual tea, she poured a generous helping of squash into a mug and topped it up with hot water; she craved sweetness for some reason and put it down to earlier events playing havoc with her body's nervous system.

Balancing the mug on the arm of the bench she sank down and leaned back, gazing out over the garden. She couldn't see any real distance because of the hedge on the far side of the main road, but she was grateful that all that was visible was greenery against the rough stonework of the houses. It had been warm all day and the walls of the cottage at her back radiated heat, it soaked into her joints and they relaxed still further.

Almost as good as a massage, she thought.

Watching the garden she saw it spring to life after her entrance, she began to hear the minute sounds of nature; bees and wasps hovering near the open flowers of honeysuckle and fuchsia.

She spotted small creatures making their way tentatively across the gravel in search of some tasty morsel to eat, and birds, she heard the birds chattering away to each other as if in some packed AGM, each one struggling to make its voice heard above the others.

The longer she sat, the louder it became, the aural trick, was, she knew, just because she had tuned everything else out, but all the same it was pleasing to think that she was being treated to a scene that few people ever saw, perhaps this show had in fact been cast and created with only her audience of one in mind.

Every so often the peace was shattered by a vehicle on the main road but on the whole they were infrequent, although occasionally a small group arrived together coming from both directions, she imagined traffic lights synchronised at each end of the road with the intention of creating this passing of traffic in this particular spot.

The events of the morning seemed very distant, as if they had happened to someone else entirely, and she was beginning to be able to view them with detachment, observing them from the sidelines instead of being in the fray. Recognising her stupidity at swimming alone, she resolved to add a little note in the book of information for future guests reminding them of the dangers and recommending that if they chose to swim, they should make sure they went with someone else and that at least one was a VERY strong swimmer, better yet, that they didn't venture out of the area where they could touch the bottom.

Her week was half way done and the place was melting into her, something that had seemed similar to an urban sprawl early on, now held its own charm and beauty and she wasn't sure she could ever leave. But leave she must, there was work to be done and her own home to return to. She still had many things to sort out and paperwork that needed attending to, but for now, for this small window of time, she could just rest and forget.

Closing her eyes once more, the sounds of the garden and of the road disappeared completely. With only a small hiccup of noise to remind her she wasn't actually asleep, she retreated inside herself and gave her mind over to imperfect day dreams.

Thirty minutes later, the sky had clouded over and she was feeling cool again. She got up to go inside, but as she moved she spotted a face watching her from behind the thin hedge that separated her from her neighbours.

There was no way of telling how long the child had been there, nor how long she had been watching and she smiled. The child smiled back, waved and then ran indoors to its mother.

She was still smiling as she took her cup into the kitchen. On the whole, given her experiences, it had been a good day. She was being treated to ever increasing insights into her psyche and that was a good thing. The guilt she felt was as strong as ever, but at least she no longer felt as if it were actually all her fault, she was beginning to apportion responsibility appropriately and she felt lighter for it.

Hungry again she put together her evening meal of rice, salad and tuna. A glass of Ginger Beer at her side and she was ready to eat, she was relieved to note that no more spiders had chosen that particular day, wall or cottage to end their days in, at least none that she could see and she finished her meal without interruption or disturbance.

After eating and washing up and although her muscles still ached from their morning's exercise, she decided to go for a walk. She would pick more blackberries, adding them to the growing pile that was gathering in the freezer. Rather that eating them while she was here, she would take them home and make crumble with them at the weekend which would be a great way to continue the pleasure of her week after it were all done and dusted.

Grabbing a plastic bag from the kitchen cupboard and promising that she would replace all those she had used with a new box from the local shop, she tested the dampness of her trainers; they were still wet and would be uncomfortable to walk in, therefore summer shoes it was and she wasn't planning on walking anywhere that would be difficult underfoot. The key slung round her neck she ventured out into the lane, but instead of turning left, she turned right and walked over the little bridge and on to the main road.

Rosemary realised she had barely noticed the stream when she had arrived, but since the rain of the previous day it was now belting along over the rocks and stones that were heaped in and around it. There was quite a flow and the sound it made accompanied her along the road in a direction she had not been before. She was certain she had seen on the map that there was a road that looped off left towards the beach and that there was a well marked track she could follow that would bring her back eventually to the road she felt she was beginning to know so well. She walked steadily for about ten minutes but no road appeared on her left and she was just about to give up and turn around when a familiar car came round the corner and stopped just in front.

'You look much better now m'dear' the voice said winding the window down.

'Thank you, I'd had a fright and you were so kind but I forgot to catch your name'.

'That u'd be Nick then'.

He smiled, encouraging her to share her name too.

'I'm Rosemary'.

She stretched out her hand and he did the same.

'You going for a walk then?' He glanced casually at her plastic bag.

'Mmm, I thought I'd find a road down here that would take me around the top of the beach area and back again, but clearly I've read the map wrong'. She smiled ruefully.

'Are you looking for blackberries too?' He nodded towards the bag in her hand.

'I was hoping to add to the collection I have in my freezer, yes'.

'Ah, well, if you carry on here a bit longer you'll come to a right hand turn, take that and then turn right onto the track immediately past the old house you'll see there, the blackberries will fair leap off the bushes at you.'

'Thanks, I will'.

With a quick nod of his head, he wound the window and was off. She watched him again as he turned off the road and down towards the beach.

Obviously he lives there she thought.

She carried on along the road as instructed and sure enough came very quickly to a right hand turn with a large house standing at right angles to the road on its corner. It was a very quiet and peaceful spot and the house, although it looked as if it had been well loved, was now empty of life. It was clear from the lack of ornaments on the window sills or pictures reflected in the glass panes that the owners had left. But there was no 'for sale' sign up so she assumed it must have been bought and the new owners had yet to take charge.

Buoyed up with a new adventurous spirit that was welling up inside her, she decided to go and have a peek through the windows.

Opening the gate carefully, just in case there was someone around, she walked through a small but perfectly formed front garden and across the front of one window to the far side.

It was as if a child had drawn the house, the door was placed centrally and there were two large casement windows either side with a room beyond each. Above were three windows symmetrically placed.

She peered into the room furthest away from the road, it was large and square with a great stone fireplace in the middle of the outside wall. It was empty of furniture. Wandering back towards the gate she looked through the textured glass of the front door, she could just make out a long straight hallway with stairs rising from the middle and at least two rooms behind those at the front. The window closest to the road looked onto a room that was a mirror image of the first.

The house had the feel of something that was newly abandoned, and she surmised that it was only recently that the owners had left. The windows were still clean and dust had not yet had time to gather, the garden was well kept and the grass, though long, was still easy enough to mow.

Emboldened by the lack of occupier, she strode confidently into the back garden and immediately spotted a magnificent Victorian style conservatory on the back. It was timber too, well maintained and painted a bright white with none of the uPVC plastic that abounded these days. The owners had clearly loved this house.

The back of the house comprised another large square room that housed the kitchen. Not all the furniture had been removed and a pine, well-scrubbed kitchen table stood as a central island amidst the modern chrome and cream appliances and cupboards.

She longed to get in and see if the inside felt as good as the outside, she was curious as to what the bedrooms were like too and imagined the bathroom to contain a wonderful roll top bath. Disappointed that it was sold, she returned to the road and continued along her walk.

Rosemary turned as instructed on to the track behind the house and sure enough, blackberries fair jumped out at her and soon she was wishing she had brought more bags with her. A return trip was going to be necessary.

She followed the track all the way along, noting the newly forming sloes and elderberries too; at the back of the garden there were apple trees planted and with no one to pick them they had fallen to the ground to be eaten by the local wildlife. The word 'haven' sprang to her mind.

She was pleased to note that the lane eventually brought her back out on her own lane, further up to be sure, but it was a great circular walk and soon she was back in the kitchen of the tiny cottage, washing her gathered hoard of berries and popping them alongside the others in the small freezer. At this rate, she would have enough for several crumbles, and a pie or two as well.

It was almost dark by the time she finished and instead of making tea and sitting on the sofa, she decided to go straight to bed with her book. She gathered up her mobile phone too and with a camomile tea in hand, she retired for the night. Turning the phone on, it pinged several messages for her.

The first was from her assistant, Jan.

'Hope you're enjoying hols see you soon J x'.

She smiled.

What would she do without Jan?

She sent a quick message back to let her know she was ok.

She opened the second message, 'I miss you. X'.

He was persistent she had to give him that, despite everything that had happened he was still hovering in the background and she supposed that at some point during the next couple of days she would need to sort all that out in her head too. She turned the phone off, not wanting to be disturbed during the night.

The book was a welcome relief and she lost herself once more in the story, surprised again to note the similarities between this story and her own.

She marvelled again at her soul's ability to state its need through her fingers, plucking the very book that would make most sense to her in that place, at that time, from the shelf and then recognising the fate that had placed the book just so on that particular bookcase too for her to find it.

God certainly moves in mysterious ways, she thought.

The two central characters had encountered others able to see them behind the facades they presented to the world and who acknowledged the reality of both their situation and the world that had caused them to create the masks they presented. She thought back to the last text, maybe there was hope that something could be salvaged after all.

Finishing her drink Rosemary was soothed by the magical properties of the herb and the honey she had added. The book she placed gently on the chair beside her bed and turning out the light she wriggled further under the duvet and watched the shadows as they danced in the various corners of the room before once more allowing sleep to overtake her.

Chapter 10

An observer, looking in from the outside would have concluded that theirs was a happy marriage and that they seemed perfectly suited to one another.

In public they were supportive and generous of the other's needs, little gestures implying that they were still 'very much in love'. It was easy because they were rarely in public together, they attended the odd event organised by their respective employers and celebrated their wedding anniversary at a different restaurant each year.

Their annual holiday was usually a week somewhere in the British Isles for James disliked travel and was queasy even at the thought of flying. Once they ventured across the channel to France, but it was such a nightmare when James was trying to communicate with the locals to buy groceries and order meals that they never tried it again.

Wherever they went on holiday, they followed a similar routine to that of home, up and out of bed by seven thirty, showered and breakfasted by nine as this time they lingered a little longer over their respective cereals and toast; and then into the car for a trip to some landmark that had been recommended by the requisite guide book bought as a Christmas gift for Rosemary by James the previous year.

They always chose to go for a small bed and breakfast, sensibly priced in the mid-range. Not for them the luxury of a hotel or the cosiness of a cottage. There was no opportunity for Rosemary to linger by a pool or indulge in a steam room or hot tub.

In fact, the idea was so alien to her, that years later, when a group of girls had suggested a week away at a spa to celebrate the impending nuptials of a colleague she had at first refused and it had taken them several weeks to convince her that she should come and that she would enjoy it.

They were right, she did and discovered a love of the lifestyle that didn't have her up, dressed and out by nine am, instead she discovered the simple pleasure of simply reading for an afternoon or tea, taken in china cup on a terrace overlooking lawns.

She started to indulge this new found pleasure and once a year would take a weekend with a friend or two and they would travel to a hotel on the coast somewhere and just laze about, have massages and relax.

James was not happy when she took these weekends off, but his argument that they cost too much carried little weight, she was spending her own money that she earned from her increasingly important positions in the local authority.

He became sulky and withdrawn before she went and always continued this behaviour for a week or two after she returned.

In fact, the truth was that he had come to despise her. She had held such promise; she was to be the Pierrette to his Pierrot drawing him gently out of his shell and wake in him a love of culture and of the arts. Together they would venture out into the unknown world and discover new places and people.

When they had first married he had seen in her a rebelliousness that he had wished all his life to have, he hoped so much that she would encourage him to become more adventurous, instead she committed to the vows she made, including the one that stated 'to obey' and had instead become docile and agreeable, accepting his every dictum and word as if it were a gospel to be adhered too. So when she discovered the gentle freedom of weekends with friends, he resented the fact that he didn't do the same and made her life as difficult as he could with his expectations of all meals cooked and ready to be heated before she went the house immaculate and clean sheets on the bed.

He never appreciated that she was young; only just 21 when they married and she'd never really had a boyfriend before, had not been to university and was still a product of her parents' upbringing. She'd never had the opportunity to develop an adult personality and her only role model was him for he was older than she by several years and she assumed, wrongly as it turned out, that he was worldly and wise. It never occurred to her that she could contradict him or that she might be able to voice her opinions and whenever she happened to disagree with him over some point of politics or news story, she kept it to herself.

Ten years sped by and soon they were both making excellent money, he had become a senior partner with his accountancy firm and she was a senior personnel manager. The house was perfect, the garden was immaculate and everything ran like clockwork. Every weekend James washed the car while she baked cakes and biscuits to last through the following week, on Sundays his mother came for lunch and on Fridays they had sex.

That their life lacked spontaneity was mostly down to James. He was shy and retreated, now that his hopes of being rescued from this predicament by his new wife were shattered, into himself even more. He withdrew into numbers and schedules and in this way he gained a measure of control over himself, his life and his wife.

Life together was driven by schedules; work schedules, gardening schedules, house improvement and maintenance schedules. It created order, there were things that need doing daily, things that were done weekly, monthly, annually and slowly the routine became even more fixed.

Two cups of coffee before leaving the house in the morning for work, two slices of toast for breakfast with the toaster set to number four and two scoops of jam on each slice; the household bills were divided equally between them and each put the same amount of money into their joint account every month. They saved for home improvements, holidays and retirement too, there was a nice little nest egg building up.

And so it happened that all Rosemary's life became measured in units. Unfortunately though, much to James chagrin, she never quite balanced because occasionally that rebellious nature of hers would stick a finger up over the parapet and do something strange like buy a cushion, just because she liked its texture.

He lived in permanent fear that she would leave him, for although he despised her, he knew that if she went he would be lost completely.

And then his mother died.

It was January 2000 and she had suffered a massive stroke from which she never recovered. James had expected to feel devastated when she eventually passed, and was curiously relieved when he wasn't. It was so matter of fact that the emotional significance of his new status as 'orphan' was completely lost on him.

The impact was felt mostly by Rosemary, who was suddenly aware of the change in their routine, no longer were there regular suppers or Sunday lunches to endure, she experienced a profound sense of freedom and couldn't help smiling all through the funeral service, hiding it behind a strategically placed hankie when she noticed people giving her strange looks.

His mother's will left everything to James, as he had known it would and with the house sold and the assets from his father's investments he would be a wealthy man; they would be a wealthy couple, and when an opportunity came up to move with his firm down to Dorset, they threw caution to the winds and returned to the county of Rosemary's birth.

She found a job quickly, with the same local authority she had started her career in. This time though she entered the office as a Senior Personnel Officer, fully qualified and with a team of her own reporting to her.

There had been massive changes in the structure of the whole organisation in the time since she had gone, but there were still enough people around who remembered her and who welcomed her back, glad to see the woman she had now become.

She acquired a nickname, Rosie, and she found she liked it and so she became a person with two identifies. She was Rosemary at home and Rosie at work, James was never aware of this split because he never rang her during office hours and chose not to attend the authority social events. She started going out alone and found she enjoyed her own company more and more.

While she made friends and expanded her circle, he became ever more reluctant to go out and despite having a large team at work, was never seen in the pub or the local restaurant they all descended on for lunch on Fridays. He was aloof and not particularly approachable and as a result no-one approached him.

Her parents had not figured much at all in the first ten years of their life together. Fortnightly phone calls and a two day visit at Christmas had seemed to satisfy everyone. Even though there was now an opportunity to spend more time together, Rosemary was loath to fall into the regular pattern that had governed her years in the Midlands with James' mother, preferring instead to drop in, unannounced or to suggest a shared supper during a phone call.

Every so often she would collect both her parents though and they would go out for the day to a local country house or garden, enjoying tea and cake in the restaurants at least as much as the fresh air itself. James rarely came along, preferring instead to work or potter in the garden and as a result he was the last to notice the changes that were occurring in his wife.

They were subtle at first; a few exotic plants in the garden picked up from independent nurseries, the odd original painting added to a growing collection in her study, a blanket thrown artfully over the sofa and a preference for picking blackberries. Each hinted that she was growing up and that finally her personality was beginning to develop and assert itself from underneath the yoke of his dominance.

It was only when she started attending the yoga class though that he finally sat up and paid attention.

Chapter 11
Wednesday

Rosemary could tell from the quality of the light in the bedroom that it was early. It still had that rosy tinge to it which lingered from the first rays of the sun touching the land. When she opened the curtains the warmth streamed in and with it a smell, a scent of autumn that spoke of soft earth and harvest, and creeping nights with log fires and chestnuts. She breathed it all in and it filled her with a deep sense of peace, knowing that this was how it had always been and how it would always be in the future. Nature was constant, man, by contrast, was not.

In the few short days she had been in Cornwall, she had grown to love this room with its curved ceilings and rounded edges.

It was a room 'with corners' as her mother-in-law had been fond of saying, which was full of character despite its simplicity.

The walls were painted the colour of clotted cream which gave it a homely feel that belied the sumptuousness of the bed and the comfort of the duvet.

The night had passed quietly, no dreams that she was aware of had intruded upon her slumber and she was refreshed and ready to face the day.

The traumas of the previous morning were gone and she thought about the day ahead of her with pleasure. She would go to the coffee morning just to see what it was like, but before she went she thought she might visit the church first. She had not been to that part of the village yet, having confined herself to the lane and the main road as far as the village hall. She was curious because she could see the church tower from her walks down to the lighthouse and from outside the village, but as soon as you ventured past the crossroads it simply disappeared from view.

Although she was not a great church goer only attending at Christmas and Easter enjoying the sense of mystery that surrounded those times of the year; she did feel at home inside the ancient buildings.

The instant she passed through their doorways, she felt calmed and soothed, and she imagined that this was as a result of the countless others who had passed that way for solace in the years preceding her. It had been a solitary shared interest between her and James, he loving the history, seeking to find out the facts of the place and she loving the feeling it invoked in her.

The walk was marked only by the presence of yet more ripe blackberries, ready for picking and she was minded to take a slightly different route back on her return to harvest the berries that lay on a different lane instead, preferring to leave these bushes to the native inhabitants, either human or animal.

The sun warmed the side of her face and her left arm, leaving her right side and arm in shadow, it pleased her to think that on the way back the feeling would be reversed and she would have benefited from the rays touching both sides of skin, producing Vitamin D and other essential nutrients that her body needed to function.

Despite not being able to see the church she knew from the map that it lay to the left hand side of the road and up a lane of sorts, she assumed that it would be signposted in some way because the tower wasn't visible from the main road for most of the distance.

She walked past the village shop, the village hall and spotted a doctors' surgery and the school. Really, this village was better served with facilities than many of the larger ones she knew of in Dorset. It was break time and the children were in the playground, running and screaming, having fun. It was a positive sound to hear and one which lifted her spirits still further.

At the far end of the school was a road, handily called Church Lane and Rosemary made the natural assumption that perhaps this might lead to the church and proceeded to walk up its steep incline.

It was bounded on either side by terraces of stone houses and it ended at the base of a Cairn. The church, if it were indeed there, would not be much further on. Her assumption was further clarified when she spied an entrance gate and long drive over hung with trees that sported the sign 'Vicarage' on the wall at its side. Next to it lay the church, out of sight by virtue of the trees in the Vicarage garden.

It looked well-proportioned and of the landscape, fitting neatly into a crevice dug especially for it from the base of the small hill that the graveyard bounded. Looking carefully she could see that the hill had been excavated, quarried probably and wondered if this were the stone that had been used to construct the building. It wasn't, as she had expected, ancient. In fact it looked Victorian, perhaps it had been rebuilt or perhaps there were additions to it.

The door was open, as was usually the case in country churches. CCTV and invisible tagging played their part in preventing thefts as much as anything else and she appreciated the gesture which allowed people such as her, free access to the buildings.

Stepping inside she was hit by the aroma of cool stone and dust, the same smell that pervaded thousands of churches across the British Isles. It became evident fairly quickly that there were no additions to the building and that, according to the information sheet; it had in fact been built less than two hundred years previously. She could have been disappointed, but wasn't. The building was beautiful, it was a simple stone cross, that was large and airy but without the fussiness one tended to associate with a church constructed by the Victorians. The altar was adorned with two large vases of sweet peas which added a lighter fragrance to the usual smell.

Walking carefully, so as not to put too many footprints on the red carpet, she walked to the altar rail and knelt down. She didn't normally pray like this when she visited churches, preferring to sit in quiet contemplation in a pew, but for some reason she was drawn to the sanctimony that the act of praying might afford her.

Looking at the cross on the alter she thought long and hard about James, visualising him in her head and imagining the hand of God sweeping across his brow, lifting away the hurt and the pain.

She asked for forgiveness, not of anyone in particular, but from whoever happened to be listening in. What had been done could not be undone and she alone had to live with everything that had happened.

She pushed herself up off her knees and bowing her head to acknowledge the power the place offered she headed towards the door, stopping to put a couple of pounds, brought with her specially, in the donation box located in the wall.

Outside the sun seemed to shine even brighter and she felt uplifted, as if her prayer had been heard and was in the very process of being answered.

Slowly she made her way further into the graveyard that surrounded the church, stopping every so often to read a headstone and in doing so, imbibe the story that went along with it. Saddest of all to read was that of the couple who had died within months of each-other aged in their seventies whose only son had died aged just nine months. To have lived an entire life without children that were desired must have caused such heartache. Even she had found it hard, the older she got, not to regret her earlier decision. However, she recognised that there had been a reason she hadn't wanted children and those reasons were as valid today as they had been in her twenties.

She carried on walking; eventually reaching the very edge of the graveyard that was enclosed by a stone wall attempting to prevent the rest of the land from encroaching further still. Looking up at the cairn she sensed the age of the land around it, recognising that little had changed in millennia and that man, who lived here now, were simply the latest in a long line of intrusions upon the landscape. Turning, she walked back along the front of the church and to the road heading back towards the village hall and the coffee morning that was taking place within.

The village hall was transformed from what she had remembered on Saturday. Bunting festooned the entrance and the beams inside, there were tables set with four chairs each dotted all around the room and stalls with a wide variety of crafts and cakes at either end. It was buzzing, there must have been at least fifty people in the room and the noise offended her ears, which had become used over the previous few days to a much lower volume. She looked around trying to spot Liz, feeling shy because everyone in the room knew each other and she knew no-one. Just about to give up, retreat and head back to the cottage she was hailed from behind.

'Rosemary, so glad you could make it, come and have a cup of tea and I'll introduce you to some people'.

Liz gently manoeuvred her into a chair and pulled another one up beside it.

The other women looked at her expectantly, she smiled and they smiled back. They all started talking at once, asking whether she was on holiday and if so, were she enjoying it; commenting on the weather and offering her a biscuit from the plate before them.

Liz took charge and introduced her to the assembled ladies. 'This is Rosemary, I met her yesterday blackberrying and she's on holiday staying in the old seeker cottage'.

A cup of tea mysteriously arrived at her side and she was grateful for the distraction that drinking it afforded her.

How quickly I have become unused to company, she thought.

The conversation ebbed and flowed around her, occasionally she answered a question directed at her but mostly she just listened as the ladies gossiped their way around the village. Liz smiled at her and squeezed her arm as if to say, you're doing just fine. But all of a sudden she felt a need to be back in the cosy solitude of the cottage.

She finished her tea and caught Liz's attention. 'I'm going to look at the stalls and then I'll walk home'.

Liz smiled again and Rosemary was struck by how confident she was.

'Of course, perhaps I'll see you again out walking before you leave'

'That would be nice'. The compliment Liz had paid her was apparent and she was grateful.

The other women acknowledged her departure and said goodbye, returning quickly to the subject under discussion. Purchasing a couple of small cakes, just to show willing she exited the hall and returned home. For some reason she was absolutely exhausted and longed to be able to flop down on the sofa with a huge mug of tea and the peace and quiet of the cottage surrounding her.

It was cool in the stone interior, the thickness of the walls meant that little heat was allowed to penetrate and that which did come streaming in through the windows was caught, keeping the chill out and a constant temperature in. Tomorrow would be her last full day so she turned her attention once more to the work she had brought with her. Apart from a few journals and industry reports she had not yet had a chance to look over; she had completed everything apart from the presentation.

Hauling herself off the sofa, she pulled her laptop out of its case and switched it on, while it was sorting itself out she made another drink and brought it back to the small side table that had served her well throughout the past six days, acting as a support for tea, plates, tissues and anything else she felt she needed close by.

The computer finally worked out its issues and was ready to go, remembering the data stick that Jan had prepared for her she retrieved that from the laptop bag as well, plugging it in she reviewed the documents and files it contained and started to construct the basics of the session she would be giving to her team the following week.

Rosemary was proficient in the use of PowerPoint and worked quickly, creating bulleted lists as necessary, adding in statistics to emphasis a point or two and including graphs she created from the excel files also located on the data stick. The presentation she was creating would serve a dual purpose of providing the notes the team would need to take away too, preventing anyone from having the excuse of not paying attention to what she was talking about. Not that she worried about this too much, her sessions were usually jolly affairs because she sought to include everyone in the room, encouraging debate amongst the team and this would be particularly important with the latest developments in their workload.

It didn't take much more than two hours to construct the whole session and she was preparing to finish when the question of the copyright notice came up. There was a standard format for any materials created within the council, but the presenter, or creator, was also expected to acknowledge themselves within the standard footer. Her usual style was to put her full name, Rosemary Edwards, but for some reason she was drawn to putting in the nickname she had been given by the team when she had returned to work. Rosie Edwards.

She rolled it round in her head. It felt good, a statement of who she really was and with a shock she realised that in a little over five days she was more of a Rosie than a Rosemary.

When she was little her mother had called her Rosie and her father had called her Rosie-Rose, but when she had met James she had introduced herself as Rosemary and the name had stuck. He had called her Rosemary ever since and she had come to think of herself as that person.

Rosemary, it seemed, was dying and Rosie was taking her place. Confidently she pressed the save button on the computer and sealed her fate forever, wondering if her colleagues would notice the small change she had made and then realising that the more perceptive of them, like Jan, definitely would. There would be a few comments made; perhaps she ought to have her name badge changed too ….!

She played with the name in her head for the rest of the day, coming back to it when she wasn't being distracted by something else. There was no doubt about it; Rosie seemed young and fresh whereas Rosemary had a matronly and definitely middle-aged tinge to it. James would not be happy with the changes she was making, and then she remembered that it didn't matter any more because he would never know that Rosemary had become Rosie.

By now, it was mid-afternoon and she remembered that she had promised herself a longer walk this morning. Her original intention had been to visit the church, go to the coffee morning and then head off towards the coastal path down one of the side roads she had regularly passed but never traversed. The plastic bag she had packed earlier that day into a pocket was still there, ready and waiting, just in case there was a harvest available and she made her way once more down the lane that had become so familiar.

The first time she had walked this way it had seemed like quite a distance and she put the fact that it now took no time at all down to both familiarity and her increasing fitness levels due to the walks.

She was quickly at the village shop and turned right towards the sea; dawdling along she spotted even more wild flowers including some favourites from her childhood, Michaelmas daisies. The scents and sounds as she walked were heavenly and she was lost in the moment, appreciating where she was for what it was and not expecting anything else at all.

The bushes were full, as they had been on every other lane she had walked down and she wondered whether the locals had so much to choose from that they never picked where she had been because there was definitely more than enough to go round, in fact she'd rarely seen such abundance before.

This time there were the beginnings of sloes and elderberries too, they wouldn't be ready for picking for another month at least though and she wondered, not for the first time, who would be the lucky people staying in the cottage at that time.

Following her usual pattern, she picked from only one side of the road, just one or two juicy berries here and there, soon enough though her bag was full and it was with difficulty that she held it closed.

There were few people on the road as she walked; an elderly couple out for a walk, a bloke walking a dog and a few cars heading towards the lighthouse and the view it offered of the wild Atlantic sea. With each of them there was a murmured greeting, a nod of the head or a raised hand.

I feel just like a local, she thought

She probably looked like one too for she carried no bag or rucksack just a key slung round her neck on a lanyard and bag full of blackberries in her hand.

The visitors probably envy me, living in such a spot, just as I know they do in Dorset.

Her reverie was interrupted by a car horn tooting hello and she stopped to take a look, it was Nick.

'Hello again' she said when he wound the window down.

'That looks like a great bag o blackberries you got there m'dear' he smiled and nodded at the bag in her hand.

She offered it out to him and he took a small handful, cramming them into his mouth, she watched as a small runnel of juice missed and ran down his chin from the corner of his mouth. He had clearly enjoyed them.

'Would you like the bag?' She offered it to him, 'to say thank you for rescuing me the other day'.

'Not at all m'dear, I have all the time in the world to pick blackberries if I want to and I wouldn't deprive you of the pleasure'. He smiled and she smiled back.

'Well, I'll be on me way'.

He wound the window up, waved a cheery goodbye to her and was off, heading towards the lighthouse once more.

Rosie thought about the people she had met, they had been lovely, it was the same in many rural areas; they had the time to stop and say hello and weren't driven by deadlines and schedules as they were in the city.

It was noticeable though, even in her little country town, the difference that time meant to those that lived and worked in town and those that lived and worked in the countryside. She had grown up with this dichotomy of time and had simply accepted that twelve o'clock meant more like two o'clock to some but it had driven James to distraction whenever people turned up late for appointments or to supply trades to their home.

It had become easier when they moved to Dorset for her to be the one that took time off to wait at home because she would just take work home with her and carry on uninterrupted until they arrived.

Jan would change her diary so that there was no one booked in to see her and the whole team had her mobile number should they need to speak to her. She couldn't see what the problem was; it just needed a little bit of organising that was all.

Eventually she reached the end of the lane she was walking on and found herself at an intersection with the lane to the lighthouse. She had two options, she could either turn left or continue down towards the sea or she could go home. She weighed them up and in the end it was the weight of the bag of blackberries which settled the dispute, not really liking the idea of carrying them all the way down the hill, only to have to carry them all the way back, she turned right and headed back towards the crossroads and the cottage.

Once back in the kitchen she followed the same procedure on every other occasion, washing the blackberries thoroughly, sealing them in a plastic bag and then adding them to her growing collection in the freezer. She looked at the hoard with pleasure; she was going to enjoy those when she got home.

She didn't fancy sitting on the sofa, nor did she feel like going to the bench in the garden, so instead she took a mug of tea upstairs and propped herself up with pillows. From her position she could see right across the fields towards the sea. The sky was mostly blue, with a few light grey and white clouds that gave a pleasing contrast to the brightness. The open window allowed the sounds of the garden to infiltrate the room and she listened as sparrows and finches sang their songs lustily across the landscape.

James came into her head again and this time she allowed him to settle and stay. It was right that this be the case as she had slowly allowed herself to think about everything that had happened in the days she had spent in Cornwall.

Growing more confident she had begun to open the door to those parts of her memory she had closed shut firmly over the last twelve months and now was the time to let the genie out of the bottle. But it had to be managed and need not be all at once, she didn't want to be overwhelmed again as she had in the near past.

She thought of him as she had last seen him. Tall and thin, almost gaunt looking with a haunted look in his eye and his mouth a thin line of deep red against the white of his face.

There was no point in wondering where it had all gone wrong, for it had always been wrong. They had never talked, James and her, about the things that really mattered to either of them and that had caused a gulf that couldn't be bridged in the end, each looking in different directions to satisfy the emotional needs that weren't being met in their marriage.

Rosie was able to see clearly how she had contributed over the years to the place that they had both come to and she wondered if her husband had been able to see his part too, or whether he had simply blamed her for not being the perfect wife. Not that it mattered now, it was over and there was no turning back. The past, as they said, was another country and one that she no longer had a passport to visit.

In the end it had been sex that had killed their marriage, that once a week on Fridays, never in the mornings, never on Saturdays or Sundays. It had come to represent a life without spontaneity without passion. It was a mechanical process that they performed because they were expected to and because they were a respectable married couple. It might have been better if they had simply acknowledged that there was no spark and they had decided to sleep in separate rooms and foregone the once weekly endurance of the soul, but no, they had both hung on doggedly to the end.

Her regular weekends away had been enlightening to say the least as she was introduced to another world where men and women, even women and women, met on equal ground and enjoyed each others company. Not that there were ever any men in the group that gathered each year, but every one of the women attending were married or in a relationship of some description. She heard their stories, played out year by year and came to realise over time that it was her and James that were out of step with the real world, that being married so young and with so little experience had actually hindered them.

Slowly, over time she had felt able to contribute small elements of her own story to the conversation and in doing so had gained the ability to start questioning the life she was living.

It wasn't, she discovered, that she was doing anything wrong or bad; it was simply that most people at least talked or argued if they didn't agree about things, bringing them in to the open eventually. James was rather proud of the fact that they never argued, she realised that it was because she chose not to provoke him and wasn't in fact the positive attribute of a successful marriage as he suggested, but an example of how well she had allowed him to control her.

What surprised her friends was that this was the case at home. Rosie, as they thought of her was feisty, independent of spirit and fun to be around. She had a sharp sense of humour and could always be relied upon to help out when needed. They did not recognise the person she was describing to them, the person that never questioned anything, that longed for holidays in exotic locations but settled for a wet week in Devon.

Few of them had really spent any time with James, they had met him of course at the odd wedding they were all attending or on the very infrequent occasions he could be persuaded to join in a meal at a restaurant, they had assumed he was shy and that he had his own friends and pursuits, they never imagined for one minute that he might be so alone as to have only Rosie.

Through her friends probing Rosie came to realise that there might just be another way and so she had started attending a weekly yoga class.

Her train of thought was interrupted by a shout from next door. 'Lily, no, I told you to put that down, you will hurt yourself'.

The mother's voice held a tinge of fear to it and Rosie climbed off the bed to have a peek out the window to see what was going on. In that moment, the child screamed in pain and she could see the young woman rushing to gather her up into her arms holding a hand that was streaming blood.

Lily's screams were becoming louder and louder and were full of real pain and Rosie was in two minds what to do next.

She pulled the window down and called through, 'is there anything I can do to help?'

The young woman looked up surprised and Rosie could see that she was crying too. 'I don't know' she was clearly quite shocked.

'Hang on, I'll be down in a second and come round'. Rosie was down the stairs in no time and reached for her summer shoes and grabbed her key.

She rushed out of the door pulling it to behind her and headed for the gate. Turning immediately into her neighbour's garden she opened their gate and headed up the path. The pair had gone inside and she hesitated on the threshold of the open door before pushing it further open and walking in.

The room she found herself in was littered with toys and she was amazed that one tiny home could contain so much to entertain two such small children. Her immediate assumption was that it would be dirty yet as she looked more closely she realised that although every surface contained a child's ornament of some description what lay beneath was gleaming and shining, clearly cleaned every day. The carpet underfoot was thick with more toys and yet there were no pieces of paper or balls of dust in corners. This young woman was a model of household industry.

She noticed tiny drops of red on the floor leading to a door on the right and following them she came into the kitchen. Old, but serviceable units surround three sides, the floor was flagged and the work surface wood scrubbed clean and free from clutter. On the draining board sat the girl her shoulders heaving with quiet sobs. Her mother was holding her hand underneath a running tap and she appeared not to have noticed Rosie's entrance.

'Is there anything I can do to help?'

Rosie repeated the question she had called from the bedroom and mother and child both looked round in her direction.

'Um, I don't know really, I don't know how deep the cut is'.

The woman looked very young indeed, too young to even have two children perhaps, but that was maybe just her vulnerability showing through.

'Let me have a look'.

Rosie moved to the draining board and took the child's hand from its mother withdrawing it from the stream of icy water. The cut was deep but clean edged and probably wouldn't be a problem if the implement that had made it was clean too.

'What did she cut herself on?'

'An old pair of shears I shoulda put away. Will she be Ok d'yer think?'

'She'll need a tetanus injection, just in case; unless she's recently had one and perhaps the doctor should have a look at it too. Can I give you a lift to the surgery or the hospital perhaps?' Rosie offered the child's hand back to its mother and smiled encouragingly.

'Thanks, that'd be great, I don't have a car you see'.

Rosie had seen on the way in that there was no car parked in the space at the front and suddenly realised that she'd never once noticed a car parked there. She hadn't really paid attention before, assuming that it was out with whoever was using it, she'd forgotten that there were still millions of people who existed on public transport alone.

Bundling the child into the back of her car with its mother and ensuring that they were both belted up took another ten minutes. Since the accident the child had not said a word and simply sobbed quietly with the pain, heaving great breaths every now and then.

Rosie retrieved her car keys and handbag from the cottage and locked the door behind her. Manoeuvring the car carefully she backed out on to the very narrow lane and turned the car around so that it was facing up the lane.

'Where am I going?' she enquired of her eldest passenger.

'The surgery will be shut so I s'pose it must be the hospital in Penzance, is that ok? The woman was clearly concerned that such a long trip might no longer be on the cards.

'Of course, it's not a problem but you'll have to direct me as I don't know where I'm going'.

Rosie headed for the main road and turned off at the crossroads back the way she had driven on the previous Friday, towards Penzance. She was excited, in the middle of another adventure, although she was careful not to let this show to her neighbour who might be concerned that this was the case for their driver.

It didn't take long to reach the outskirts of the local city and fortunately the hospital was well signposted. In no time at all the pair were deposited in A&E, with the details of Rosie's mobile number so that they could call her when Lily was ready to go home.

She left them to it and headed right out of the car park and assuming that if she went downhill that she would be going towards the harbour she followed the narrow streets and one way system, hoping to find somewhere she could leave the car and go off to a café where she could sit and have a coffee perhaps. She'd grown a little tired of tea all the time and was definitely in need of a change.

Her hunch proved right and eventually she found herself facing the seafront, turning left without any idea of where she was going except that it looked as if there was more going on in that direction than towards the right, she drove slowly along.

Very quickly she came to some sheds clearly for the harbour and spotted a couple of cafes and a pub.

There must be a car park somewhere along here soon, she thought.

She carried on travelling slowly for there was no one behind her, over a small swing bridge and spotted the harbour car park almost immediately on her right. Turning in, she parked in the first available spot and got out to shove money into the ticket machine.

She looked over to her left and saw that there was a shopping complex handy.

I can always find somewhere there if necessary she thought and then turned resolutely back the way she had driven.

Walking over the swing bridge she went past the RNLI charity shop and towards the cafes she had spied as she drove past. The first she came to on her left didn't look open and she carried on, until she arrived at The Boatshed, a friendly looking place playing a song she liked not too loudly on their music system. There were plenty of people sitting drinking and eating both inside and out and she felt that this would be as good a place as any to while away the time until she was needed as a taxi service once more.

Heading to the counter she asked the woman making drinks if she was able to just order a coffee.

'Of course you can love, what would you like?'

The smile she received was big and warm and genuine and Rosie liked her immediately.

'A latte please'.

'You go and sit down and I'll bring it right over to you'.

Rosie picked a small table for two just by the front entrance where she could watch the cars passing on the road outside and in no time at all had a large latte sitting just in front of her; it was made with full fat milk.

Sod the detox; I need this, she thought.

She glanced at the clock on the wall it was just after seven o'clock. She tried to work out how long she had been lying on her bed and couldn't. Her stomach growled and she remembered that she hadn't had anything to eat since breakfast. Well, the coffee was a start at least. Thinking that she might be in for a long wait she went back to the counter to order something to eat and enquire as to when the place shut. Knowing that she could stay for another two hours was comforting, after that she would need to find a pub to hole up in and not for the first time Rosie regretted not bringing anything with her to read. She would just have to sit and stare at her fellow coffee drinkers.

Rosie didn't really fancy a full meal and settled for a simple starter instead, goats cheese with a tomato salsa on a bed of leaves and when it came she tucked in. The flavours burst in her mouth and danced around her tongue and she was reminded of just how boring it was doing detox. This would be the perfect treat she mused and quickly mopped up the rest of the food.

Her mouth occupied, her thoughts could turn once more to James and she was just getting settled when her phone rang beside showing an unknown number that she assumed must be the hospital. Picking it up, she flicked it on.

'Hello'.

'Rosie, is that you?' the voice was hesitant on the other end of the line, expecting her to hang up she thought.

'Yes, it is'. Her answer was short and succinct, not wanting to give anything away.

'It's me.'

'Yes, I know ….. What are you calling me for?' She was aware that her tone was less than friendly, but after the evening she was having she was not in the mood for chit chat, preferring to get him off the phone as soon as possible.

She was suddenly aware that she had hurt him and more gently 'I'm sorry, that was uncalled for its just been a bit of an odd day, that's all'.

'I just thought I should tell you I love you, just in case you've forgotten while you've been away'.

His voice conjured up an image of his face before her, bright blue eyes, sincere in their emotional intensity, open and caring and she struggled not to start crying.

'Thank you, I think I needed that, it's been quite a few days but I think I'm getting there.'

'Good, I'm going to go now, I just wanted to hear your voice, you have no idea how much I miss you.'

'I miss you too and …….' she hesitated over the words '…. I love you too'.

The silence on the other end of the phone was long and made her worry that she had inadvertently cut the call off and then his voice came back.

'You have no idea how long I have waited to hear you say that to me Rosie'.

There it was again, that name, Rosie, an acknowledgement stronger than any other she might have had that she was a newly emerging person.

'Look I have to go' she said 'I'm waiting for a neighbour to call me'. 'I'll see you on Friday, yes?'

'Yes, I'm looking forward to it so don't forget to let me know what time to pick you up'.

'Ok, I won't, bye'.

She put the phone down regretting almost immediately the words that had left her mouth. What had she done? They had been out before she could stop them and she had no way of unsaying them now. Well, she'd just have to live with the consequences.

Her phone pinged, one new message received. When she opened it, it was simple and concise 'Thank You X.'

As there was nothing she could now do, she returned to her reverie and thought once more about her marriage.

Rosemary's weekly attendance at the yoga class had caused quite a stir in the Edwards household. On Tuesday and Thursday evenings she no longer went straight home from work to cook an evening meal, instead she visited the local leisure centre for classes lasting an hour and a quarter.

Assuming that the class would be easy she discovered much to the shock of her muscles that it was in fact, quite difficult indeed to form even the most simple of forms and stances. She persisted though and over the course of a year or two had become reasonably proficient, moving from the beginners' class to the intermediate and finally the advanced.

She also discovered an entirely new set of friends, separate and distinct from her work and childhood friends who looked at life even more differently than the others and consequently than Rosemary herself. They spoke of retreats and spiritual journeys, they visited Glastonbury and walked to stone circles and they took themselves off for healing and mindfulness sessions, reading books by Carolyn Myss and Paolo Coehlo.

As her attendance at the yoga class progressed so did her own personal journey, she became increasingly aware that life was not necessarily something that needed to be endured and that she had more of a say in its outcome than she had previously thought possible. She too began to attend classes and courses that were beyond her normal run of the mill activities; she learned to chant and meditate and practiced yoga at home in between her regular classes.

James was not a happy man; whilst his wife's development into adulthood had largely passed him by up to this point, he could no longer ignore the fact that she was becoming a completely different person and that she wasn't taking him along with her either. She was passing him by and he was fading into her distance.

Rosemary wasn't aware that he felt like this for he never commented on her activities and never asked her what she was doing or how it had gone or even if she had learnt anything new. As far as she was concerned it seemed he just ignored it completely, choosing to forget that these particular days and times existed in the week, jumping straight from Tuesday morning to Wednesday morning completely missing out Tuesday evening altogether.

When she got home from her class he was inevitably in bed even though it was only eight thirty. He would have eaten the meal she had prepared the night before and retired almost immediately after he had washed the dishes. It did not occur to him even for a moment that he too had an opportunity to do something he might find interesting, that he too could, if he wished go to the gym or a class or even for a walk. Instead he sulked in the same way that he had sulked when she went off for her weekends away with her friends and Rosemary capitulated by ignoring his sulking, choosing not to make an issue of it or even call it to their joint attention. Perhaps if she had things might not have turned out the way they did.

Rosemary was not by nature selfish and it would be wrong to assume that she did the things she did deliberately to provoke or annoy James, but it would be fair to say that on occasions, perhaps once or twice a year that she would book herself into a workshop or a conference that would cause him to feel that he must comment.

'What on earth are you dong that for?' seemed to be the most common of these, followed closely by 'You are becoming quite mad you know, no serious person could possibly think like that'.

If they had been used to a marriage where open debate were encouraged then such questions might have been the opening statements into some interesting discussions where both could air their opinions and laugh together at where they differed. But they didn't have such a marriage and the comments were simply designed to wound; a limp attempt to get Rosemary to change her mind and to return to the stability, as James saw it, of their previous existence.

As a person she was growing. But that growth never extended into her relationship with her husband, she still didn't question him, choosing instead the path of least resistance which therapists would probably have described as passive aggressive. She simply informed James what she was doing and added it to the family calendar which hung in the kitchen, nodding in agreement whenever he chose to make one of his rare comments about her life.

It had never occurred to her that she could use her adventures as a way of opening up their relationship, probably because she had never realised that he had hoped she would be his salvation, his rescuer from himself.

While Rosie was thinking about the long term effects of her life choices she had been drinking her coffee and it was with a start that she noticed her cup had been drained and that another was probably needed. The counter was empty of customers and now seemed as good a time as any to purchase a second cup.

Returning to the table she gazed out of the café across the darkening car park and towards the harbour, Lights sprinkled the edges of the quay reflecting in the water beyond and adding a slightly surreal, fairytale atmosphere to the town.

She examined herself internally, how did she really feel right now?

Was she able to make a real assessment of her situation or was she simply reacting to being in a different place.

Rosie was unsure of the answers to these questions and aware that they were important to her future decided to file them away for another time, perhaps a time when she had finally laid to rest all the ghosts of her life thus far.

Her phone suddenly sprang into life, an insistent tone that demanded answering. Holding the receiver to her ear she heard her neighbour on the other end telling her that they were ready to return home now. Assuring her that she would be with them in just a few minutes, Rosie closed the call, drained the last of the coffee and headed back across the bridge and now empty expanse of car park to her car.

Deciding it would be simpler for her to carry on along the sea front until she picked up the main road again, it took no more than ten minutes to return to the spot at the hospital where she had deposited the pair just a couple of hours earlier.

Lily's hand and arm were heavily bandaged presumably to prevent her from picking at the wound. She was sleepy and her eyelids were closing as she cuddled into her mothers arms. Swiftly deposited into the back seat both mother and daughter looked vulnerable and young, a glance in the mirror assured Rosie that all was well though and a rare smile emerged from her neighbour.

'It was good of you to bring me 'n Lily to the hospital, I don't know how to thank you' the woman spoke softly, not wanting to wake her daughter up.

'It was my pleasure, it really was no trouble at all', speaking the words, Rosie was surprised to find that she meant them, that they weren't the usual sentiments spoken but rarely sincere used to oil the wheels of conversation and society.

'I'm Ginny by the way, I forgot to tell you in the rush and this here is Lily'.

Rosie suddenly remembered that there was a second child, a baby too. 'I've just realised that we didn't bring the baby, I hope he's OK'.

'He's with his granny for the night, once a week he goes and tonight is the night' Ginny smiled again, 'he's good he is, especially for his granny'.

'Doesn't Lily go too?' The question was asked before she had time to think about it and she regretted it almost immediately fearing that it would be taken as prying.

'Different Granny', the reply was given matter of factly without any trace of shame or justification.

'Oh, I see'. Rosie was embarrassed, she didn't know what to say, she knew that there were many women who had children by different fathers but had never actually met any of them so wasn't able to understand how it came about, other than by the actual mechanics of course.

'He's not mine only Lily is mine I'm his aunty, Aunty Ginny. His mum, my sister works in Truro so I look after them both, she'll be back later on. It's a long day she does today'

'Ah, I hadn't realised, in fact I don't think I've heard anyone but you in the cottage next door'

'A thick wall, that's what it is, Ellen works late so sleeps in, I expect you will have been out on your walks when she went out.'

Her comings and going had clearly been noted thought Rosie.

The woman in the back smiled and closed her eyes and the conversation, such as it was, ended.

The drive back to the village did not take long and in a very short time they were all safely ensconced back their various residences with promises of coffee in the morning exchanged between herself and Ginny.

It was almost ten pm and rather than turn lights on, Rosie headed straight to the bedroom. It had been another tiring day, this business of relaxing was not as easy as she had thought it might be and her mind was still whirling through the conversations she'd had in the café and the car. In amongst it all was James and her recognition that she had been the person that had changed, not he. Poor James, he had been an unwilling partner in her personal development.

Teeth cleaned, she climbed into a bed which welcomed and soothed her, as her head touched the pillow she had one last thought before drifting out of consciousness.

Where was James right now?

Chapter 12
Thursday

Her last full day in the cottage began with a loud crack that woke her from a night of disrupted sleep. The clap of thunder was almost immediately accompanied the flash of lighting and was the precursor to the curtain of rain which now began to hammer at the side of the tiny cottage, clamouring to get in to shelter from the torment that the wind wrought upon it.

Rosie drifted in and out of consciousness; it had not been a good night. She had not slept well and the bed which had been so welcoming and comforting to begin with had become a place of torture as she struggled to find some comfortable position that would enable her to drop off to the sleep she so desperately craved. It was not to be, and she had spent the night turning over the events of the past and those of the week she was in with the question she had posed herself the night before. Unable to get tunes and snippets of song lyrics out of her head, she had driven herself crazy with the constant repeating of a line or two for what seemed like hours at a time.

When it became clear that she was not going to get what she needed she conceded defeat and trudged downstairs to make a hot drink. Eschewing the camomile and honey she preferred at night, she opted for the caffeine of Earl Grey, well aware that this could probably add to her difficulties, but not caring, simply needing the comfort it might provide. Her mug contained the tea bag and her milk, it was topped up with hot water when the kettle pinged off, the tea bag was fished out and the whole lot was taken back up to the bedroom.

Sitting in bed she nursed the cup, enjoying the heat from the mug in her hands.

'Asbestos fingers' James had called her and she never minded. Sipping the tea, she toyed with the idea of getting her book out to read, the story was coming to an end and Rosie was well aware that if she didn't finish it today, she probably never would. She decided against it, preferring instead to simply sit, drink tea and allow her mind to wander, she was wandering anyway and a book probably wouldn't stop the thoughts from coming unbidden into her head.

Once more she was thinking about James. He had been so handsome with a striking figure and tall and when he smiled he could light up the whole room. It was a pity he rarely smiled though.

As she remembered, she realised that his life had not turned out as he had hoped it would, not that she could be certain about his hopes and dreams because they had never discussed them, they had not discussed hers either, but she had been fortunate enough to be blessed with an outgoing personality and a friendliness that had endeared her to others ensuring she always had friends.

With a shock it dawned on her that she had been James' only friend, she struggled to recall others who had come into his life; male company or female for that matter and noticed that there had been a lack. He had never been one for sport, he didn't watch football or rugby and you couldn't call him one of the lads either as he rarely drank, preferring a single glass of wine on their occasional evenings out. He'd had no interests it seemed and whilst this hadn't mattered in their early years together as they had slowly built the life that became their prison, he hadn't developed any later on either.

James, she reflected, was not the man she had thought he was when she married him. But then again, she was not the woman he had possibly thought she would be when he married her too.

By now she had finished her tea and carefully placing the mug on the floor by the side of the bed she snuggled back down under the duvet and closed her eyes. This time she fell asleep only to be woken with a shock several hours later by the storm which arrived in full from the Atlantic.

Rolling on to one side Rosie remembered that today would be her last full day and she felt bereft as if something precious had been taken away from her. Today was also the day when she would do what she had been intending to do throughout the week but had failed to do so far.

Climbing out of bed, she made for the shower and full wakefulness. In little less than half an hour she was dressed and her hair was dry. The little cottage was warm downstairs, clearly the storm was not succeeding in clearing the air and there was a strong scent of rosemary mixed with lavender when she opened up the front door to test the temperature outside.

The rain continued to fall unrelenting into the ground, hammering its notes through the glass and the granite and she ate her breakfast watching droplets gather and fall down the window panes at the front of the house.

She hadn't practised yoga in nearly twelve months and was suddenly moved to do so. She had no mat but that was simply an inconvenience, she found a copy of the yellow pages on the bookcase and decided to use that as a block for her head.

Moving the sofa back towards the dining table, she had enough room to do a basic routine and lay down with her head on the yellow pages and drew her knees up to her chest. Rosie allowed her shoulders to fall back to the floor, conscious that they had started to rise up towards her ears again and gently rolled from side to side, massaging her back and easing out the aches of the night she had just passed.

Her back began to loosen and she rolled over on to her side, swinging her left arm in a wide arc around her head back to her side, rolling to the other side she repeated the movement with her other arm. Her shoulders complained the muscles had not had this sort of stretching for many a month and were unaccustomed to the use.

She moved onto her front and with her arms supporting her bodyweight practised the sphinx position, this had been one of her favourites from her regular class and she was disappointed to notice that she could not longer push herself right up. Instead she settled for resting on her forearms as her back relaxed into the stretch. It was a short movement from there into the cat and the arching and rounding of her back made her feel good.

Finally she pushed herself up off the floor and into mountain steadying her left foot firmly against her right leg she put her hands in prayer position and lifted them skywards. She stood in this way for what seemed like hours but was probably no more than a few minutes before putting her leg down, shaking out all over and then repeating the process with the other leg.

When she had finished she felt much calmer, more able to face what lay ahead and had become aware that the muscles which had become looser over the course of the past few days were looser still, a sure sign that she was almost as relaxed as she was going to be. She glanced out of the window, the rain had finally stopped and the clouds were clearing away slowly leaving behind a brighter cast to the sky than had previously been the case.

Putting her cereal bowl and spoon in the sink was the final act she undertook before she headed out on her, now customary, walk. Turning left out of the cottage once more she walked down the lane and across the road at the end. However, this time when she headed along the lane opposite she didn't carry straight along towards the lighthouse; instead she decided to walk at an oblique angle in the opposite direction to any she had previously taken.

The narrow road would take her down to another hamlet; she could see it quite clearly and had been able to all week but had not felt moved to venture there before. The coastal path ran straight through its middle and she headed off confidently in a completely new direction.

As she walked she noticed things to which she might not have paid heed twelve months earlier, such as the quality of the light. It was amazing that the direction in which one walked could have such a profound influence on the way that light bounced around the landscape before settling on the retina to create the perfect picture she was now observing.

Not only was the light different walking in the opposite direction to her usual route, but the sounds and smells were different too. Wondering at what may cause this change in so small an area Rosie came around a bend and spotted the change in the landscape immediately.

To her right were the familiar hedgerows and fields rolling gently down to the cliff edge to which she had become accustomed over the last few days. Blackberries adorned the hedges, Michaelmas Daises poked though the crevices and birds raced and darted, calling to one another as they picked up flies and other insects driven up from the ground by the force of the rain.

To her left though was a vastly different story. The land had been raped and shorn of any semblance of country to make way for mine workings that were still clearly in use. Tin sheds dominated the skyline as she looked back towards the village and she marvelled that she had not been able to see them on any of her previous walks; they were clearly well concealed from the view of the majority. It was such a pity that those who walked the coastal path were the only people that would see this insult wrought upon the earth.

Abruptly she was reminded of her earlier analysis of a landscape as raw as any inner city sprawl and realised she was probably looking at what constituted a significant proportion of the local economy.

Noting this, she was reminded of a conversation that had taken place some years earlier between her and James where he had patiently explained the mysteries of economics in local society to her.

For all his faults, he was knowledgeable about such things and was able to discern the important facts from the wider story, distilling everything down to its key component parts and then explain them in ways that others would make sense of and understand themselves. He was a good man; he had never intended their marriage to be as barren as it was no more than she herself had either.

This line of thought brought her back to the present; she still had a job to do, but had yet to find the will to do it. It was almost as if something needed to happen that would allow her to make the final break but Rosie had no idea what this might be.

She decided to carry on walking. For the time being it seemed like the most important thing in the world and as there was nowhere else for her to be it also provided a solution to her current state of unknowingness.

As she walked she remembered more of the man James, the man whom she had married over twenty years earlier, the man she had met on Waverley Station during an early attempt to assert herself in the world, the man she had vowed to obey and who had slowly become the man who was a burden to be with.

All the time she was thinking these thoughts she was reminding herself that it had not been his fault, it had not been either of their faults, everything had happened because of their combined unwillingness to talk about what ailed them and their marriage. It was strange really because here she was now, twelve months on talking to herself and laying all bare and she was determined that the same mistakes would not be made a second time.

She rounded another bend and noticed that a lane ran off back towards the main road. By this time Rosie was getting tired and shading her eyes she looked towards the sun peaking through the remaining clouds and surmised that she had been walking for at least an hour or more and that maybe this lane had been provided at just the right time for her to do a circular walk back to the cottage she now thought of as home.

The lane looped around the far side of the mine workings, passing a number of cottages and houses that had obviously been built during the heyday of the village. They looked mostly empty, not of furniture as such, but of life. They were probably holiday homes, packed up for the summer with perhaps another week to go during the next school holiday before standing unwanted and neglected over the winter.

Sadness washed over her, they deserved better these little places of cosy homeliness; they deserved to be loved and not lie abandoned. Winter would probably be harsh as there was little to stop the direct exposure to the elements with no trees or hills to act as barriers and it was clear that little could be grown. She knew from her own childhood though that such places also had a rich life of their own during the cold of the year where locals made their own entertainment and shared the warmth and friendliness of nights spent playing games, telling jokes, watching visiting films and acting out in plays.

She wondered what it might be like to live in the village permanently, to leave the comfort and familiarity of Dorset and to enmesh herself somewhere brand new that didn't know her and where she might be able to explore this new person she was developing into, Rosie.

Rosie too was an orphan, her parents had both died within a few months of each other just a couple of years earlier. They had left everything to her, as she had known they would and this additional wealth had added handsomely to the Edwards family coffers.

She had done nothing with her inheritance simply allowing James to manage it as best he thought, recognising that he was better suited to the job than she and also acknowledging that it gave him a great deal of pleasure to look after her interests in this way. It was almost as if he were able to fulfil one of the roles he had set himself in life, one which she had taken away from him by being successful in her own right, that of the 'provider'.

It was an archetypal role and all men were raised to believe that it was their responsibility to take care of the financial needs of their family ensuring they were housed, fed and comfortable to the best of their ability.

James had provided this role to his mother when she were alive and had, to some extent, helped her parents out too, although with two of them it was less important that he be involved. He had also taken on the role with Rosemary too, encouraging her to let go of responsibility at work, hoping she would decide that the life of a mother and wife would be enough to satisfy her but sadly reminded daily that it would not.

Perhaps, she thought, she might use some of the money to buy herself a small house here. She savoured the thought for a few minutes until she realised that it would be unfair on the house as it too would lie idle and unwanted for most of the year only springing to life when she had a mind to visit Cornwall.

Dismissing the idea as unworkable she turned her attention to her surroundings instead. The cottages were giving way to open pasture land once more and she finally noticed that the fields were much smaller than those of her home county; they were bounded by dry stone walls rather than hedgerows most of the time. The hedgerows were mainly reserved for the sides of the lanes. She wondered at the difference in size of field and assumed it had something to do with the fact that crops could not be grown in the stony earth and that only very hardy animals would thrive in such conditions too.

Eventually she reached the main road once more and turning left headed back towards the village and her cottage.

She had not gone far when a car stopped on the other side of the road and Liz popped her head out of the window.

'I know it's short notice and I'm glad I spotted you, but would you like to come to a quiz night this evening in the pub?'

Rosie was unsure of what to say, on the one hand the thought of going to the pub on her last night was the thing she was the least likely to want to do, preferring to stay in and savour her remaining hours; on the other hand having a little company might help to break her reverie and prepare her for her re-entry into the world tomorrow.

'Yes, thank you, I'd like that'. She answered firmly

'Excellent, seven thirty at the Fox, do you know where it is?'

Rosie had passed it several times on her daily walks and so nodded her head to indicate she knew it.

'I'll see you there' she said and Liz smiled at her, waved goodbye and carried on driving in the opposite direction.

When she got back to the cottage she was tired but reasonably happy, she was almost looking forward to going out that night, although there was a niggling doubt in her mind about the wisdom of such a move.

Never mind she thought, if I don't enjoy it I can always plead a headache or packing to do and leave early.

In the kitchen she made herself a sandwich and a cup of tea. She took both to the bench in front of the house which had by now dried out from the rain.

Sitting quietly Rosie contemplated all that had happened over the last few days, reflecting that she had changed in some profound and magical way into the Rosie she now saw before her.

She had arrived Rosemary and now couldn't even remember who that person was. She thought of herself as Rosie and was minded to mention to Liz that night that she was, in fact called Rosie too.

As she sat she was reminded of the last time she had sat in such a way, with a cup of tea and a sandwich in front of an old stone cottage on a bench much like this one.

Chapter 13

It had been raining, hard; much like the day had been in Cornwall today; great lashings of water hitting the pavements and buildings asking to be let in. In amongst the rain were the gashes of lightening that bolted across the sky in magnificent arcs, lighting everything up out of the September gloom that sat squarely over the town and surrounding countryside.

Rosemary was mindful that the steps outside the council building were treacherous at the best of times, even more so when they were wet and she was wearing heels. She grasped the rail hard as she made her way as quickly as she could to the car park. The umbrella held over her head was not making an enormous amount of difference to how wet she was getting.

A clap of thunder came suddenly with no warning and she stumbled, falling down the remaining two or three steps and hitting the ground with a hard bump and a fair degree of pain.

She sat shocked, not noticing that she had let go of the ineffectual umbrella as she fell and was now getting steadily soaked through, her light mac was not enough of a barrier to prevent the water from making its cool way to her skin beneath the dress she was wearing.

Rosemary became aware of a pair of arms hauling her up off the sodden earth and reached out for her briefcase to prevent it being left behind. She was carried carefully back into the reception hall of the council building she had just departed and set down on the comfortable chairs visitors awaiting appointments usually occupied. She looked up into the eyes of a gentle man, how she knew he was gentle she didn't know.

Perhaps it's his eyes, she thought.

He smiled, she smiled back.

'Are you OK?'

The concern was evident in the words and the voice that carried them, she was reminded of the time that James had spoken those very same words all those years ago on Waverley Station and began to cry, not huge racking sobs, just a light sprinkling of tears that belied how tired she felt and the amount of pain she was just beginning to notice.

A hankie was proffered by Jean who was behind reception and she reached for it gladly.

'Thanks' she said, sniffing slightly to hold back the snot that was threatening to run.

She turned back to her saviour, 'I don't think I am actually, my foot feels like it's been run over by a bus'.

She held her ankle out for inspection and was pleased to see that the pain was justified by its ballooning nicely from all sides.

'It looks like you might need to go to a hospital or the doctor and get that seen too'.

She nodded her agreement and looked towards Jean.

'Can you order a taxi for me please Jean?'

'You will do no such thing' the words he spoke were forceful and not to be contradicted, 'I'll take you in my car, it's only along the road and won't take any time at all'.

'Really, you don't have to do that, I don't want to inconvenience you any more than I already have done' she spoke quickly as she glanced at the rest of his appearance, it was clear he had got muddy and dirty picking her up off the floor and he was wearing a suit which suggested he might have been about to go into a meeting.

'It's nothing that can't wait' just a query with the planning officers over some development land and I can come back later to deal with that'.

He smiled and held out his hand 'Adam, Adam Smith'

'Any relation?' She enquired. He had clearly heard the same question many times and shook his head.

'I'm afraid I'm a humble builder and no philosopher' he smiled as he spoke the words and then added 'I'm told that Smith is a very common name'. His eyes had a hint of laughter around their edge and she laughed out loud.

'Rosie, Rosie Edwards, no relation to anyone famous either'. They looked at one another again and smiled.

'Come on, let's get that foot sorted out. I'll go and bring my car round to the front and come back for you in just a moment'. He glanced her way before heading towards the door.

'It's ok I'll hobble to the doorway'. Rosie stood up and gingerly put her weight on her right leg, it gave way almost immediately.

'Ah, I think I'll wait here if that's OK'.

She watched him leave the building and make his way around to the visitors' parking area that lay to its right. She became aware that Jean was watching her and they smiled conspiratorially.

'He's nice' she said and Rosie couldn't help but agree.

In no time at all he had driven her to the hospital and commandeered a wheelchair. Pulling it to the side of the car, he helped her out and into the conveyance. Pushing her across the car park she felt a little like the Queen of Sheba but was aware that her clothes were damp and dirty, her hair was a mess and her make-up had run in the rain.

So much for Queen she thought, tramp maybe.

The staff on reception asked for her details together with those of her next of kin. She was acutely aware of Adam standing beside her when she was giving out the name, phone number and address of James' office. Throughout the whole he had held onto the back of the wheelchair and when the receptionists were done it was he who wheeled her into the waiting area.

'Would you like a cup of coffee or something?'

He glanced at the machine standing blinking in the corner, it was clear that he didn't think it was going to be good coffee; but at least it would be wet and warm and it might soothe her. The pain was beginning to intensify and she needed a distraction of some description.

Scrabbling in her briefcase she pulled out her purse and extracted a variety of coins and held them out to him, he selected a number of them and went to collect two cups of coffee.

'You really don't have to stay you know', although I appreciate that you are she thought.

'I'll just wait until your husband arrives or until you go in to the doctor and then I'll head off'. I just want to make sure you're OK.'

He really is the nicest person, she thought; I could get used to this sort of attention, and then caught herself.

She was married, had been for over twenty years, the last thing she wanted was any sort of entanglement; life was just fine as it was.

'We're going on holiday on Saturday'. She began a conversation, anything to steer things back onto more familiar and easily managed territory.

'Off to Cornwall ... walking' the joke couldn't be more apparent if she had spelt it out to an audience and they both laughed.

'At least I think it will be my husband doing the walking this time and I shall have to fill in the time as best I can'.

'Cornwall is such a beautiful county and it's my homeland originally, although I moved away as a boy when my father's job changed. I go back regularly though. Where are you going?' He spoke thoughtfully.

'Somewhere near Zennor I think; there was novel about DH Lawrence that my husband read and it captured his imagination. I've never been before and the furthest west has always been Devon You know cream teas and ginger beer, that sort of thing, from the guidebook it looks like this is quite rugged and wild, completely different to the sort of thing I'm used to.'

She spoke quickly; aware that time was ticking on, seeking a way of keeping the conversation going with this person who was making an impression upon her in a way that no-one else had ever done before.

'It has its own sort of beauty that's not for everyone but ..' he looked appraisingly at her '... I think you'll fit in just fine and I think you may even find that it suits you'.

A nurse came into the waiting area

'Rosemary Edwards' she called and several heads turned hoping that the name was wrong and that their turn had in fact arrived, but it was Adam who put his hand up, indicating Rosemary sitting next to him. The nurse came over and grasped the back of the wheelchair firmly, ready to steer it towards the more private areas of A&E.

Adam looked down at Rosemary and said 'Goodbye, I do hope your foot gets better soon.' And he walked away with a smile and wave.

Rosemary felt lost.

I know nothing about him except his name and that he's a builder.

She was aware of missing a piece of a jigsaw that she had just had a glimpse of finishing and that it was now gone again, lost in the myriad of other pieces that lay scattered on the table of life all around her.

She turned her head just in time to see him leaving the entrance to the hospital, he turned at the same time and they smiled again, acknowledging that a connection of some description has just been made and was not yet ready to be broken.

As she watched his progress she spotted James walking across the car park too, the two men nodded to each other but shared no words. He was lost to sight and she was moved swiftly round the corner into triage by the nurse.

It wasn't long before James was by her side and they were sharing the experience of her foot being strapped up. No bones were broken but it was a nasty twist and she was informed by both the doctor who examined her and the nurse that strapped up the foot that she must rest both it and herself for a few weeks, avoiding putting undue strain on the foot and under no circumstances was she to walk without the crutches that were provided.

She had assumed that James would be annoyed but was surprised to find that he was solicitous. He heard all about the story of her fall and the stranger who rescued her and brought her to the hospital without interruption or comment, gazing into the distance as if gathering his own thoughts and conclusions.

She left nothing out, she didn't want to stand accused of something that had never happened and was rigorous in the telling of the tale from start to finish.

James took charge of the wheelchair back to the car, gently lifting her into the passenger seat and informing her that he had arranged for a junior in his practice to drive her car home for her and that he would run him back when he arrived.

He carried her into the house and set her gently down on the sofa and helped to peel off the clothes that were by now less damp but still incredibly dirty. She sat naked while he retrieved pyjamas and dressing gown from their bedroom and then helped her re-dress.

She was just sitting with a welcome cup of tea when the doorbell rang, it was her car being delivered by James' junior member of staff and the two men went back into town.

Rosemary now had time and space to think about all that had happened through the day's events, aware of the subtle undercurrents that were being played out beneath the surface of the actual events themselves.

Adam, she savoured the name in her mind, running it over and around her head until it felt as familiar to her as James. It answered a call inside her, but not knowing what the call was she dismissed it as simply an over-reaction to the shock of the fall and the pain in her foot.

James brought in fish and chips for supper; she was surprised at this degree of foresight and thoughtfulness too. He had never been particularly fond of 'fish suppers' as he called them, but she adored them, revelling in their gooey softness and salty flavour and as a result they were mostly treats to be enjoyed on evenings out with the girls in her circle or when she was away for a weekend; rarely did they enter the home that she and James shared.

They sat, side by side on the sofa, she with her foot propped up on a low pouffe with a tray each balanced on their knees and tucked in. This was a shock to her system too, not for James the informality of a TV dinner, it was either a kitchen supper or a dining supper depending on who was cooking and what day it was.

The Edwards household ran on schedules and these included mealtimes. Tuesdays and Thursdays were kitchen suppers each of them eating at different times the meal she had prepared in advance the day before to allow for her yoga classes.

Every other evening of the week and Sunday lunchtimes were dining suppers taken in the dining room with a full compliment of cutlery, matching crockery and wine glasses; these suppers comprised at least two courses with coffee or tea each according to their taste afterwards.

On occasions there would be other ad-hoc kitchen suppers provided, when her parents were invited over for instance or when Rosemary was away for a weekend. At times like these the radio was left on; Radio 4 as it had been during her childhood and there was an easy conversation that took place.

Dining suppers by contrast were mostly silent affairs, broken only by brief enquiries into the minutiae of each other's day, snippets of office gossip and change shared in an effort to make all feel the way that normal married couples feel.

Whilst they ate the fish and chips brought in by James, they talked about the upcoming holiday discussing whether it was still wise to go or not. The decision was that yes, they would go and that James could walk if he wished and she would take a pile of books she had been looking forward to reading, they could still share trips to local villages and towns that they were both looking forward to seeing as long as they were suitable for her crutches and this they could ascertain from their hosts at the bed and breakfast they had booked into.

The following morning James headed off to work as usual with promises to call the bed and breakfast people to check that she wouldn't cause a problem with her crutches. Rosemary lay in bed in a vain attempt to fall asleep again but long years of rising by seven thirty every morning had instilled an inability to enjoy this unexpected opportunity.

Sighing she sat up and swung her legs to the side, grasping her crutches firmly she hopped over to the en-suite and ran a bath, another indulgence that was rarely enjoyed in the Edwards household, recognising that she would not be able to stand in the shower to wash herself.

Rosemary added a generous measure of the very expensive Rose Otto bath oil that had been a Christmas present from her mother the year before she had died and gingerly let herself slide into the bath. It was only when she was laid down that she realised she might not be able to get out again.

Ah well I can just keep topping up the hot water until James gets home at lunchtime if necessary.

She closed her eyes and allowed the water to rise up above her belly and her breasts and let her mind drift. This was not a familiar experience for Rosemary, she was normally careful not to allow any dissent of her thoughts to appear anywhere in her psyche lest she feel that she had been short-changed in some way. It was true that her workshops, courses, yoga and weekends away had opened her eyes to a completely different way of living, but she never for a moment considered that this way might be open to her.

She was still two different people; at home with James, she was Rosemary and at work and with her friends she was Rosie. It had never occurred to her that she was both and that she could have both if she so wished.

As she lay in this way images rose in her mind's eye and she was granted a rare glimpse into her life from a completely different perspective. She watched again the drama that played out in her life from the first moment she had met James to the present day, she finally recognised that it was the need she had felt to get away from her parents' influence that had led to her marrying James in the first place and whilst she felt no regrets about this became acutely aware that somehow she had missed other opportunities.

She watched as her life became split in two; her life with James creating one half of the person she was and her life at work creating the other half of the person that she was. It wasn't James' fault that this had happened and she recognised that there were things about herself that she failed to understand.

The images flowed and there was an acknowledgement in them that everything was connected, that her life was the sum of the decisions she had made and not made. Finally, she settled on the day before, her accident and the image of Adam's eyes came up before her and the recognition that what she felt had passed between them was something more than was obvious from the surface.

Rosemary drifted in this way for a long time and when she came too the water was uncomfortably cool. It was time to attempt to get out of the bath or to top up the water with hot. She chose the former and putting all her weight on to her arms pushed herself up onto her left leg, not for the first time she was glad she had been doing yoga for so long, she was much stronger than she looked.

Hauling herself onto the side of the bath Rosemary reached for the towel she had placed nearby earlier and then holding onto the side of the bath she slid round and was out.

Sitting on the loo she dried herself carefully, paying attention not to rub her right ankle too firmly. Replacing the strap that had been removed for the purpose of bathing she was once again able to move about with the aid of her crutches. Hobbling back to the bedroom she chose some loose knitted cotton trousers and a warmish cotton jumper.

They were going on holiday the following day and no packing had yet been done, now seemed as good a time as any to lay out the clothes and other items that would be necessary for their week's stay. She had the advantage that everything was reasonably close to hand which would reduce the amount of exercise she needed to take using the crutches that were going to be her constant companions.

Underwear was retrieved from the drawers nearest to the bed, socks as well just in case it were cool, although she would only need single socks she reflected as there was no way she would get anything on over the ankle that had now swollen to twice its size. Loose trousers were probably going to be all she would be comfortable in so several pairs of differing colours and textures were added to the bed next to her, short and long sleeved t-shirts and three comfortable jumpers completed the clothing selection.

Pyjamas, a nightie in case it was hot and a dressing gown came next and finally her wash bag filled with the essentials that occupied her normal routine at home each day. There was no need for make-up, they wouldn't be going anywhere that required it and besides her ankle, she was now recognising, had provided her with the perfect excuse to have the sort of holiday she had always wanted; slow paced and relaxed with plenty of time for reading and tea.

She smiled to herself as she added a pile of books to the growing stack of stuff on the bed. James would sort himself out, he always did and he would retrieve the suitcases too, he was good like that. He hadn't needed mothering in the way some of her friends' men needed looking after, he was quite happy in the kitchen or with the washing machine; she had been lucky she thought.

The effort to get everything sorted out over Rosemary became aware of being tired and in pain again, clearly the pain killers had worn off and she needed some more.

Bugger, they were in the kitchen.

She had forgotten to ask James to bring them up for her, she would just have to make her way downstairs to get them and she could then settle herself downstairs on the sofa with a good book.

The stairs proved easier than she had feared, simply sitting down she shuffled down on her bottom one stair at a time, using her left leg to propel her along and guide her descent. Her crutches were moved along at the same time and when she reached the bottom it was as simple as standing straight up and into the arm rests provided.

Their kitchen was a large farmhouse style that reflected the old Georgian house they lived in perfectly. Gleaming white units topped with black granite surrounded her on three sides, the chrome and black of the electrical appliances contrasted beautifully to her mind and not for the first time she was pleased with the overall effect, it was her favourite room which was one of the reasons why kitchen suppers were her favourite meals.

The dining room was too fussy for her taste and besides it was on the other side of the house too far from the kitchen for comfort. It had been decorated with formality in mind which was why dining suppers were always quiet affairs as if both she and James were intimidated by their surroundings.

The tablets she had been given at the hospital were next to the sink and she took two quickly. A cup of tea would be welcome now and she would drink it at the farmhouse table, that way she didn't need to worry about how she would get it to the sitting room.

Sitting once more and unoccupied by activity her thoughts returned to the images from the bath, there was no denying that her life was her doing, she couldn't blame anyone and if it needed to change then she was the only person who could change it. She had never thought before about how her life might change and the thought that she and James might not be married any more was alien to her, but now that it had been raised Rosemary was unable to remove the thought from her mind.

What would it be like to be free, she no longer had to worry about her parents' feelings, they had both died the year before, she didn't have to worry what her friends might think as they were constantly amazed that Rosemary and James were still together anyway, the only person she had to consider was James himself.

Once again the image of Adam came into her mind.

Why do I keep thinking about this man I don't know, what is it about him that I find so inviting?

In her mind she looked at him all over again, from the top of his head and his amazing blue and kindly eyes down to his feet shod in comfortable brogues that were reasonably fashionable. He had been wearing a rather smart suit underneath his mac she remembered, one that fitted perfectly on his lithe frame.

Mentally, she added James to the picture, both men were handsome but each had a different look about their eyes. Whilst

James was haunted and shy, Adam looked confidently out at the world with laughter lines threatening to emerge at any minute. James rarely laughed and it was as if he had nothing to feel happy or joyful about and now that she thought about it, his eyes looked sad as if there was some great disappointment always lurking in the wings.

In the recognition of his deep disappointment she realised she would not be able to leave him. She knew that she would be there living this half life until they both ended their days. Adam was, she thought, simply an aberration - a saint who had come to her rescue when she needed it but was no longer of any consequence and she would put him out of her mind because she could do nothing about it or him and anyway he was probably married himself. These flights of fancy about changing her life had to stop.

Draining her tea she was in the process of making a second cup when she was startled by the sound of the front door slamming. James walked into the kitchen.

She was so surprised to see him that the words were out of her mouth before she could stop them 'what are you doing at home?'

He seemed taken aback by the abruptness of her question.

'I thought I'd come back to check on you and make you some lunch, I thought I'd take the rest of the afternoon off so we can get sorted out for Cornwall'.

He was defensive and she regretted her comments immediately.

'I'm sorry, I was just so surprised to see you and it's a lovely thought, thank you'.

She smiled to emphasis the words she had spoken and was rewarded with a return smile back.

He came around the table to her side and softly kissed her head. 'Now, have you had your pain killers, I forgot to leave them upstairs for you'.

'I know, I came downstairs to get them and was just drinking tea. Would you like some?'

She looked at him enquiringly and he replied 'You go and put your foot up in the sitting room, I'll bring it in to you and I'll bring a sandwich too'.

He shooed her out of the kitchen and into the sitting room and she, once more surprised at this change in his behaviour, meekly complied with his request settling herself on the sofa once more and picking up the book she had left there the night before.

James backed in to the sitting room carrying a tray that contained a pot of tea, a jug of milk two mugs and a ham salad sandwich for each of them. He placed it carefully on the coffee table and poured a mug of tea each handing one to her and taking one for himself. She put the mug down on the side table and he passed her the sandwich too, they ate.

At first she was aware of the silence between them, recognising it to be the same silence that descended during dining suppers, then she remembered the thoughts that she had been having just before James had returned and was ashamed of the fact that she could even consider leaving him, it wasn't James' fault she was the way she was and she could change her life if she wanted to.

For his part James regarded Rosemary, he watched how delicately she ate the sandwich the lightest and smallest of bites, savouring every morsel. He watched as she drank her tea and how the thoughts she was thinking were written over her face.

'I've lost her' he thought.

He had been aware the day before that she had become animated in a way he hadn't seen before when she spoke about her accident and the man who had taken charge of her predicament.

This was unusual for James as he was normally the last person to see something happening, preferring the regularity and solidity of figures than the randomness of human interaction and engagement.

He had come home early in order to fill a need that had arisen in him suddenly, a need to spend time with the woman who was his wife and whom he loved even though she had failed to rescue him from himself and his ways.

James acknowledged that he had despised Rosemary for a long time but at the end of things he realised that this was because he was not like her, he didn't have the confidence she did and that he had hoped some of that would rub off on him. It didn't of course, because we are each the masters of our own destiny and confidence needed to come from within.

However, he never said any of this to Rosemary, that was not his way and they had lived so long in their separateness that he didn't know how to change the pattern beyond what he had already done with fish and chips and returning home early. He wanted to of course, but couldn't find the way to start the conversation and the moment was lost, forever.

Noticing that she had finished her tea he asked if she wanted some more.

'Yes please, that was lovely James, thank you'.

She smiled at him as they swapped cups and he was once more aware that they were on different sides of a divide that could never be crossed.

He resolved in that moment to change things, he wasn't sure how he might do this but recognised a strong need to do so. Perhaps fish and chips in the sitting room was not such a problem after all, and maybe the occasional short day in the office or a visit out at the weekends might be the start of something new.

He understood intuitively that Rosemary would never leave him, but he found he now wanted her to love him again, to once more be the couple they had been when young before the regimen of their lives had set in.

He stood and gathered up their lunch dishes.

'I'll pop these in the kitchen and then go and start packing'.

'I've made a start on my things James, they are all on the bed, I couldn't get the suitcases though'.

Rosemary was keen to show that she hadn't been completely idle despite having a twisted ankle and James appreciated the effort she had made.

As he made his way upstairs, Rosemary became aware of a subtle change that had taken place in their relationship.

Somehow a truce had been called without any words spoken or white flags flown, it was a minute change but welcome and her heart rose and the confusion in her mind dispersed into the ether. She would never leave James and perhaps this holiday which would be so different from any they had shared before might be the precursor to a change in their lives too. She smiled to herself at the thought.

Chapter 14

The holiday started well enough. James who was taking his new persona seriously allowed Rosemary a long lie in on the Saturday morning, waking her gently with a cup of tea at nine thirty.

She had not had a good night; her foot had throbbed and no amount of pain killers had been able to provide any measure of relief. She had tossed and turned and in the end had urged James to sleep in their spare bedroom because she was keeping him awake too.

He, by contrast had slept well, in fact he had the best night's sleep he could remember for a long time. His night had contained neither dreams nor disturbance and he woke refreshed and happier than normal.

Whilst Rosemary slept in the morning he had sorted out the house, making sure it was secure for their week away; moving the pot plants to the bathroom so they could soak up water of their own accord through the drip mat system he rigged up and he filled the car with all the accoutrements they needed for their holiday, including his, but not her, walking boots.

By the time Rosemary was dressed, breakfasted and ready to go he was all prepared.

They travelled directly to their lodgings, no deviations were made to interesting National Trust properties en-route, no museums were visited and no cultural exchanges were made. This was in complete contrast to all their previous holidays together when every single possible activity was expected to be accounted for in a long tick list of things to do and accomplish.

The change had been made to take account of Rosemary and her ankle, he was acutely aware that she was in pain and he was also following through on his promise to himself to change.

On the odd occasions in the past when Rosemary had suggested that their holidays should not be quite so frenetic, he had dismissed her objections with a smart 'but we'll probably never get the opportunity again and it does come highly recommended in your guide book'.

He reviewed those past holidays and acknowledged that, at least in part, his constant desire to see new sites and sights was perhaps due to the fact that otherwise they might have to spend time together talking, and who knew where that might lead. No, it had been better to ignore the need to explore the undercurrents of their relationship, smoothing everything over with a light dusting of gloss instead, shared activities making up for the lack of shared understanding.

Despite their direct route though, they did stop frequently for coffee and loo breaks and once for lunch too. This was also a change in their normal routine for James had preferred to march on towards the next point of interest on the map picking up snacks along the way if it were absolutely necessary and stopping for the toilets only when there were none to hand at any of their guidebook destinations.

They reached the bed and breakfast a little after three. It was different from places they had booked before. This time it was in the middle of nowhere on a slight deviation from the road between St Just and Zennor. There was a village about a mile down the road and on another occasion they might have walked to the pub it held.

It was beautiful, thought Rosemary

She found she was moved by the landscape in a way she couldn't describe; just in the way that Adam had indicated she might be. Perfect, that was the only word to describe the setting.

The house had a large garden which was bounded on all sides by large shrubs and banks of enormous herbs including rosemary and lavender, it smelt breathtaking and she found herself looking forward to spending quite a lot of time just sitting and being on the bench she spied at the back of the sitting room window. She would have a fine view of the surrounding moorland and as it was at the back of the house the sounds from the main road receded into the distance, leaving her with the call of the birds and the wind.

In view of their circumstances the owners of the bed and breakfast had consented to offer an evening meal as well as the breakfast for a small additional cost. Both she and James were grateful for this concession to her ankle as neither felt that they wanted to be in a car looking for somewhere to eat each evening. On past holidays they would normally eat at whichever town or village they happened to be visiting, picking up a sandwich for later on.

Rosemary was also to be provided with lunch on the days that they weren't out visiting villages and tourist sites. James planned to continue with their normal routine and take a packed lunch out with him each day, returning to supper in the evening.

Mr and Mrs Marsh were kind and generous hosts. Mrs Marsh or Vicki as she insisted they call her, fussed around Rosemary as if she were a fragile doll in a china shop, making sure she sat with her foot supported and with tea and biscuits easily to hand.

Nothing was too much trouble and soon both of them fell under the spell of being well looked after and began to relax into the rhythm of the place.

Their room looked out over the front of the house towards the sea and the light that streamed in that first evening was tinged with roses, lending the whole room a glow that comforted and cosseted.

There were thoughtful touches here and there; a kettle with fresh milk and tea bags so they could make their own drinks, a tin full of biscuits should they need a snack in the night, lovely soft and overlarge towels in the bathroom and plenty of cushions on both bed and armchairs.

Rosemary watched as James carefully unpacked both suitcases, depositing them on top of the wardrobes as soon as they were empty. Everything was either hung up or folded neatly into their respective drawers. Her wash bag was emptied into the bathroom and her books were piled on the bedside table next to the bed.

As she watched him, she began to see the James she had known when she were younger, the James she had fallen in love with; his methodical ways and the carefulness of his movements, nothing was wasted in the way he moved, he was economical with himself as well as with everything else.

Could she repair this marriage?

She pondered the question, feeling a little at odds with herself as she did so; on the one hand she had a lifetime of experience that indicated they could easily fall into the same ways of being they had always had and yet, something had shifted. Was it enough to make a difference in the long run?

We shall just have to wait and see, she thought.

He brought her over a cup of tea and sat in the armchair opposite hers. 'Is there anything you would like to do this evening?'

The question was full of concern and she responded in kind.

'No, thank you though, my foot is really quite painful and I think I'd prefer to just sit and rest if that's alright with you'.

He indicated that it was and fell silent.

They drank their tea quietly together and for the first time in a long time it was with a sense of comradeship; nothing needed saying and no conversation was necessary. How familiar they both were she thought, we have been together for so long that we no longer need to speak.

James broke the silence.

'Would you like to go out tomorrow?'

She thought about it and nodded, actually yes, she would like that.

She would make an effort for James' sake as he would be finding the change in their routine harder than she to bear for of course she often introduced small changes into her life without really thinking about it, a course here, a day away there, a weekend with her girlfriends, even the odd cushion she bought because of its texture or colour.

'Yes, I'd like that. Perhaps St Ives maybe?'

She phrased it as a question but it was more of a statement. The chances were that she would be able to manage at least a small part of the town on her crutches and if not, then there would be plenty of places to stop and rest a while to gather her strength.

Recognising her effort James was appreciative and went to collect the guidebook that had been his wife's Christmas present the year before, checking the index he flicked to the pages about St Ives.

'Today's tour begins at the famous Tate Gallery located in St Ives. The spectacular north Cornwall coast provides the perfect backdrop to the village and its surroundings. The magnificent gallery was opened in 1993 and now provides the perfect home for a wide collection of local, national and international works of art. The roof top cafe provides the perfect spot from which to view the beautiful views of Porthmeor beach.' He read the first paragraph out to her.

'It sounds perfect; I just hope there is a lift up to the roof top café'. She smiled at him and he smiled back.

He was just about to read some more when their host, Vicki called to let them know that supper would be ready in five minutes and that she would see them in the dining room.

The following morning dawned bright and clear, once again James left Rosemary to sleep deciding instead to go for a walk before they left on the day's adventure to St Ives. Vicki had provided him with breakfast and assured him that Rosemary could have hers whenever she was ready saying there was no need to worry about the time poor thing, she needed to rest that ankle of hers and sleep was just the thing to get the healing started.

When Rosemary woke, she was alone in their room and disoriented for a moment until she remembered where she was. She glanced at the clock; it was after nine again, James would be waiting. She struggled out of bed and into the bathroom to wash herself, fearing at that he would return at any minute to chide her for her tardiness in the light of such a beautiful day.

It was only when she returned to the bedroom after her bath that she noticed the note propped up against her hairdryer.

'Gone for a walk, back soon. x'

That was a turn up for the books; she thought and took her time over drying her hair and getting dressed.

It was almost ten by the time she finally presented herself downstairs.

She was greeted warmly by Vicki and ushered into the dining room for breakfast. Choosing cereal and some toast, Vicki departed to provide it for her, returning quickly with a fresh pot of tea and some milk for her cereal.

She ate slowly, savouring each mouthful and when the toast arrived she spread it thickly with home made strawberry jam and butter, tucking in lustily, not caring that it spread all round her mouth.

Her mind wandered, as it seemed to be doing more and more these days, over the events of the last few days and the enormous change that seemed to have come over James.

What was it he was reacting too? What had caused such a seismic shift in his personality?

She was not naive enough to assume that it had occurred spontaneously but was unable to pinpoint the actual event that had triggered such a change. It was true she had had an accident but then she had been though various illnesses over the years, some more serious than others and none of these had resulted in this sort of behaviour.

Her reverie was interrupted by James return, he looked fresh and rosy from his walk and his eyes were lit up like jewels, he looked …. She struggled to find the word …. younger. Yes it was as if years had been removed from him and he was younger. He had clearly enjoyed his walk and sat down next to his wife to help himself to a cup of tea.

She had finished eating.

'Come on then, you all ready for the day ahead?'

He was brisk and to the point but she didn't feel any underlying tension in the statement and nodded her agreement.

He disappeared upstairs to fetch her handbag and she grasped her crutches and they made their way to the car with assurances from Vicki that they would have 'luverly time'.

St Ives did not disappoint. It clung to the coast like a small jewel in a brilliant setting, cobbled streets, although difficult for the crutches were taken with care and the Tate gallery certainly lived up to the description of the guide book. They had lunch in the roof top café and yes, there was a lift which made getting there so much easier than attempting the stairs on her behind.

They discovered small gift shops and galleries to linger in and ended the day sitting overlooking Porthmeor beach with an ice-cream each to hand watching the families who were packing up after a hectic day spent lolling about on the sand and racing into the sea.

It had been a good day, neither of them felt short changed in any way and both had seen the potential of this brand new life that beckoned.

They arrived back to Vicki Marsh and her husband tired and happy. Dinner was served at seven and they were in bed and just about asleep by nine thirty. This time Rosemary slept well too, the fresh air and exercise had obviously done her good.

The following days of their holiday fell into an easy rhythm; every other day would be a trip out to a place of interest or local village, somewhere that Rosemary could easily use her crutches. On these occasions they consulted with Vicki Marsh who was a walking, talking library of information about the locality they had found themselves in.

More than once they praised their good fortune at finding her and her lovely home as they discovered hidden gems usually reserved for the locals and which tourists, unless they were exceptionally lucky rarely saw.

The other days were spent separately, Rosemary resting either in their bedroom, in the sitting room or in the garden, depending on the weather and her mood to dictate her choice. She would read and sometimes chat with Vicki Marsh when she had a spare minute or two, comparing notes about their respective lives and the busyness they both contained; vastly different and yet so similar.

James on the other hand would take himself off in the car to find a part of the South West Coast path that contained a circular walk of sorts which allowed him to leave the car at one end and walk in a large loop along the sea side of the coast and then back to the car. These trips would normally last all day and he would return content that he had enjoyed the beautiful county of Cornwall with lots of pictures on his camera to share with Rosemary in the evenings.

Both of them realised that this was a far easier and more enjoyable holiday than any other they had experienced in their marriage. Each was having their needs served and they were spending time together too. Rosemary and James were astute enough to realise that perhaps this held the key to the future longevity of their life, although as was their custom, neither said the words and neither expected to discuss it. It was almost as if they were reading each other's minds without knowing that's what they were doing.

Despite her ankle, Rosemary was finding the holiday uplifting and the events of the previous week faded from her memory, surfacing only occasionally when a thought rose that caused her to compare her marriage now with her marriage of just a few days earlier. In those moments, another face would arise before her and it would look at her long and hard and she would lose herself in the blue of his eyes and wonder what life might be like if she weren't married to James.

They were due to leave Cornwall on Saturday and had just two days left before returning to their normal life, except of course that Rosemary wasn't going to be returning to work for another week or two at the very earliest.

They were having a discussion over supper about how she would manage the following week when Vicki Marsh suggested that Rosemary stay on in Cornwall, she was no trouble and there were no other guests to come and it would be nice to have the company as

Mr Marsh was out at work all day, returning in the evenings after his office had closed.

Rosemary jumped at the chance, an opportunity to stay on here in Cornwall for a few more days solved the problem of how she might manage at home and also it gave her a little more respite as she had not been looking forward to spending long hours alone in their lovely home when James was at work. Both knew that his early departure from the office of the week before had been a once only event and that he would be unlikely to be able to return home early or even during the middle of the day to see to her needs, such as they were.

It was for this reason alone that James agreed to come and collect Rosemary the following Saturday instead and to travel home alone. Truthfully, he was a little relieved, he too had been concerned about how they would cope once they were out of this small bubble of time.

As a gesture of thanks, Rosemary spent the next two days travelling about Cornwall with James, falling back into their old pattern of making the most of the sights that were available too see, with just a nod towards her infirmity being the acquisition of a wheelchair whenever one was available, which was frequently at National Trust properties and less so at others. She didn't mind this as much as she had done in previous years, she knew that next week she would not be getting out as much and relished the opportunity to see as much as possible of the world surrounding her.

James finally departed Cornwall at midday on Saturday, hoping to be home by four o'clock promising to call as soon as he arrived safely. Rosemary sat in the garden and stared out across the fields before her, there were no trees to block the skyline, just moorland with boundary walls and grass.

At four o'clock the call came from James.

'I'm home safe and sound, now you look after yourself and I shall pick you up next Saturday. I'll call tomorrow to check you are OK as well.'

He had sounded brisk and efficient.

'I'll also call the office for you on Monday to let them know that you are not in Dorset and are staying in Cornwall for another week too'.

Rosemary appreciated his thoughtfulness and thanked him profusely, a little too profusely perhaps had someone else been listening. To be honest she was glad to have this time on her own, of course Vicki Marsh would be around, but they had an intimate understanding of one another's needs as women often do and there was an unspoken agreement that she and Vicki would not be in each other's pockets.

This was the first time she had ever holidayed alone, it was true that she had often gone away without James, but that was with girlfriends or parents, she had never been alone in this way before and it was exhilarating.

The days passed pleasantly and her ankle healed a little more each day. Soon she was able to put a little weight on it occasionally and experimented with short walks up and down the garden paths that surrounded the Marsh homestead.

Despite the time of year, the weather seemed to be getting warmer too, there had been no rain for over ten days and the ground was dry and brittle, little puffs of dust rose up off the paths as she placed each of her crutches, left and right down as she walked, she marvelled at the intricacy of it all.

I put my crutch here, a puff of dust there, she wondered at the lives she was disturbing by her passing.

Rosemary spent more and more time in the garden, sitting beneath the window watching the world of nature pass by drinking tea and eating sandwiches, just being, just living and not even really thinking.

By Tuesday she had finally relaxed enough to let her shoulders come down from her ears, her face looked free and her eyes were brighter. She was benefitting from being in the fresh air and was sleeping so well that she was much less tired as well.

She was in such a pose, eating a sandwich and drinking tea when the police arrived. Two men accompanied Vicki Marsh through the back door and out into the garden. She looked up expectantly wondering what was going on.

'Mrs Edwards?' The voice was kindly and the question spoken with care.

'Yes'. She replied with a single word not wanting to hear what was coming but knowing what was coming because the booming of her heart and the quickening of her pulse in her ears told her what she already knew.

James was dead.

Chapter 15

'Are you alright?'

The question came loudly over the dividing wall that separated the two cottages. Rosie jumped and was suddenly aware that she had tears streaming down her face. She had been crying and she didn't know how long she had been doing so.

Ginny's face was a picture of concern.

'Hang on a minute I'll be round to get you. Come and have a coffee in here with me'.

Rosie was too well mannered to refuse although that was what she felt like doing and thought perhaps I need this to break the spell of the past few days and my memories.

She allowed herself to be guided through her garden and into next door.

Ginny sat her down at the table by the front door and disappeared inside to fetch drinks, appearing a few minutes later with a cafetiere of richly aromaed coffee, two mugs, some milk and a plate of biscuits, 'just in case you're hungry' she said watching Rosie.

She had also thoughtfully provided a box of tissues which Rosie now helped herself too in order to wipe the tears away and blow her nose.

Ginny chattered away, giving her time to compose herself and was very adept at feigning a lack of interest in what had made Rosie cry.

Eventually Rosie was able to say thank you.

'I appreciate you coming to get me, it was just what I needed, I'd been thinking about my husband. He died you see, just twelve months ago and I've been doing a lot of thinking while I've been here and it all seemed like yesterday'.

Rosie sniffed again and more tears welled up and spilt over her eyelashes, she reached for another hankie and gave a good blow.

'It's always best to cry when you need to' said Ginny.

'I find that it helps me cope with all sorts of things, sort of gets it all out in the open like and then I can see things freshly'.

She smiled and Rosie was reminded of the stir Ginny's entrance had caused at the farmers' market. It seemed rude to ask directly, but she couldn't help herself.

'I was at the farmers' market on Saturday and I couldn't help noticing ...' she trailed off unsure what to say next.

Ginny fortunately supplied the remainder of the sentence for her '.. that the locals don't like me you mean?'

She laughed, 'it's not that they don't like me, it's just that they don't understand me, or me sister come to that either. They never know what to say to us, so don't say anything just stare and stop talking is all'.

Rosie must have looked confused so Ginny continued.

'My husband and my sister's husband ran off together, they were gay y'see and they had married us because they thought they weren't. When we brought them together they realised that they fancied each other more than they fancied us'.

She laughed, 'it's all water under the bridge now, so long ago and we see them regularly, the kids and me, my sister even works for them and they are both good with the kids too, love having them to stay over and they bought this place for us too, give me the housekeeping as well so's I can stay home and look after Lily and Joe.'

My face must be a picture thought Rosie.

Whatever it was she had imagined in her head it certainly wasn't anything as strange as this tale and Ginny seemed so happy, so content and so comfortable with the idea that her husband had run off with another man.

Next to Ginny, her own life seemed simple and uncomplicated. She started to laugh, great gales of laughter swept up from her stomach, Ginny joined in and they laughed until they were unable to laugh anymore, until their sides hurt and their bellies ached.

The two of them spent a lazy afternoon chatting in the sun in Ginny's garden until it was time to collect Lily from school. The baby, Joe, was at his grandmother's again and would stay there until the following day. They walked together along the lane, past more succulent blackberries, along the road joining other mothers in the school 'run', until they reached the school gate.

Rosie noticed how many of the other mothers stayed away from Ginny, almost as if they though they might catch their husbands in the same predicament if they stood too closely, but Ginny didn't seem to mind and she exchanged a few words of greeting with some who were clearly braver than the majority. She spotted them also looking her up and down, obviously wondering where she fitted into the picture that was this strange family.

At that moment though there was a great deluge of children from the school, as if they had all been disgorged from the mouth of a great brick whale. Lily was in the middle of a great gang of girls, brandishing her arm about without a care in the world.

'Hello', Lily spoke to Rosie.

'Hello back', Rosie smiled down at Lily and watched her as she started to tell her mother all about her day at school. It was clear that she enjoyed it and her enthusiasm for sums and reading and making things shone through.

She must be a delight to teach, thought Rosie.

In no time at all they were back in the lane outside Ginny's garden.

'Would you like to come in again for some more coffee or tea perhaps?'

Ginny's face was open and welcoming and Rosie realised that there was nothing she would like more than to spend time in the company of this young woman who had endured so much but was still untainted by it all.

They sat, once more, at the same chairs they had occupied earlier in the day with steaming mugs of hot tea in front of them this time. Lily was engaged in important business with her dolls and toys and occasionally you could here her chatting away to them and telling them what they could and couldn't do.

'So how did your husband die then?'

The question was unexpected and direct and Rosie was unsure whether to answer or not, it seemed a bit intrusive. But then she remembered her own question earlier on and was ashamed at the thought.

She bit her lip. 'He was knocked over by a car and killed instantly in the high street at home'.

It was true; James hadn't seen the car coming and had been rushing across the road to his office on that Tuesday morning just over twelve months earlier.

The driver was devastated, it had been a complete accident, there was no one to blame but James himself but that hadn't made it any easier to deal with for anyone.

Ginny reached out and grasped Rosie's hand and she was encouraged to continue.

'I was in Cornwall, on holiday still, recovering from a sprained ankle'. She gave the facts simply despite her feelings of inadequacy.

'I should have been there, maybe if I hadn't stayed in Cornwall he might have been a little later to work and would never have been hit by that car'. The tears threatened again.

Here was the nub of it, her guilt at being responsible for James' death, however indirectly. This is what she had been building to all week as something she had to face and she was doing so with this slip of a girl who was no more than half her age, who held her hand and whose eyes said they understood and wouldn't judge her and who would just accept that this was what she needed to feel right now.

Ginny smiled encouragingly.

How strange, thought Rosie, that this is where I would find solace. This child has been through so much and still she has so much to give too.

Rosie remembered the look of concern on the police officer's face when he told her that James had been knocked down and killed. She remembered her worry about being able to get back and was told that she would be taken home by the local constabulary and that she would be taken to identify the body before going home.

She had been asked if there was anybody they could contact to be with her when she got home and she remembered shaking her head despite knowing there were many people she could call on in this, her hour of need, but none she actually wanted. The person she wanted was James and he couldn't be there because it was he who was dead.

Mrs Marsh had packed her suitcase for her, given her strong hot and sweet tea for the shock and had stayed quiet, understanding that the last thing Rosemary had needed was someone chattering away. In the end, she had given her a quick hug and said that she would keep her and James in her prayers and that she didn't need to worry about the bill, they would sort it out later. They never did.

All of this spilled out of her in a torrent, the memories that had never before been told to anyone else, the guilt she felt at staying in Cornwall, the shock she had of identifying her husband's body and the swift response of her friends that helped her arrange the funeral and deal with his affairs.

Fortunately, James had been meticulous in ensuring that everything was in order and it had all gone smoothly with no hiccups or problems to mar the transfer of assets from joint names to a single, solitary name.

Through it all though was the thread of guilt, that it had been her fault; that she had caused James to have this accident; that somehow she had been the instigator of it because she had considered a life without him and perhaps a life with someone else.

Ginny sat and listened to it all, making occasional noises to help soothe the tension, stroking her hand and making more tea.

Eventually, Rosie was done, she had said it all, she had exposed herself to herself more than to anyone else and there was no where else to hide away the truth of how she felt.

'I came here this week to scatter James ashes into the sea. This was the one holiday we had that we had both enjoyed and it would have been the one we referred to all the time had we grown old together, so it felt right that this was where he came to, in the end'.

'And have you done it, have you scattered his ashes?'

Ginny asked the question even though she already knew the answer.

'No, I don't know how to' was the simple reply from Rosemary.

The truth was that when she scattered his ashes she would be free finally and she didn't feel she deserved to be free. So the time had not been right and as a result she had not done what she had come to do.

'When Mike left me for Rob, I couldn't think. I was convinced that it was my fault, that somehow I hadn't been good enough for him, that I hadn't been a proper woman or wife and that if I could have just been perfect then he wouldn't have left me.'

Ginny spoke quietly.

'The truth was though that he had always been gay, he had used me to try to show the world he wasn't, so I could never be a perfect woman because it was never a perfect woman that he wanted. It was hard learning that lesson and the guilt I felt in the years afterwards stopped me from living and so I ended up where I am now. I wouldn't change my life for the world because I love looking after Lily and Joe but I could be doing more. I also know now, that it wasn't my fault and that I have nothing to feel guilty for'.

Her statement was easy to understand. Here was a woman who had been wronged by a man, the age old story brought right up to date with a more modern twist, yet it was she the woman who shouldered the guilt that came with that wrong, not the man. It had never been the man; it had always been the woman who had taken responsibility for ensuring the relationship worked.

Rosie mulled it over, it was a new thought and one she had not really considered before.

Her friends had told her it wasn't her fault, that it was an accident but they had not been privy to the thoughts she had been having in the days before it had happened; they did not know the way she had looked at another man and wanted him; they did not know that she had begun to consider life without James even though she knew she would never leave him.

'Thank you Ginny, for telling me that'.

She genuinely appreciated the gesture, it had been as hard for Ginny in a very different way as it had been for her and perhaps she had even had it easier because she, unlike Ginny, had the support of a large group of friends and colleagues around who didn't judge her.

It was getting chilly outside and it was time to leave. Rosie hugged Ginny hard.

'You have no idea just how much you've helped me today and I want to thank you so much for everything'.

Ginny hugged her back saying 'sometimes you get help from the strangest places and I've enjoyed our afternoon even if it was a bit heavy'.

They departed each into their respective homes, Rosie thoughtful and Ginny with her hands full of a small child's needs.

The last thing that Rosie needed that night was to go out into the company of a crowd of people, but she had said she would be there, so be there she must.

At seven thirty precisely she presented herself at the Fox dressed in jeans and a loose fitting jumper. She had eaten nothing in the intervening time since leaving Ginny and was now hungry from her long walk to the pub.

Spotting Liz in one corner with two other people she made her way through the crowd to sit down.

'Hi Rosie, glad you made it, I was a bit worried we were only going to be three on our team'.

Liz introduced her to the other couple.

'Jean and David live not far from you just along the lane in the house on the corner with that marvellous garden at the front, you know the one we met outside the first time'.

Rosie nodded her head and shook hands with them both saying 'I hope you aren't hoping for great things, I'm normally terrible at quizzes'.

They smiled at her and both said at the same time 'so are we, but its good fun anyway'.

'What would you like to drink Rosie?' David asked.

'I'll have a large dry white wine please, thank you' she replied.

He went off to the bar to collect her drink and she turned to Jean.

'Do they serve food do you know?'

'Oh, yes it will be out shortly and all the quiz players get to have sausage and chips courtesy of the landlord, we just help ourselves from the bar when they arrive'.

Jean looked over at the door at the back of the bar, 'I can see that the plates will be coming out any minute now'.

As she finished the last word, the door swung open and a woman staggered in with a huge pile of plates which crashed down on the bar counter, a second woman appeared with an enormous tray of golden chips and a third woman came through with what seemed like several hundred sausages all baked to perfection. Rosie's mouth watered at the sight and she was one of the first up to grab the fare provided.

When she sat back down again with a full plate of chips and two large sausages her drink was waiting and Liz, David and Jean were all smiling broadly.

'You look like you need that' said Liz.

'Oh, I do, it's been an odd day and the last thing I ate was a single sandwich at about eleven thirty, I'm starving'.

It was true, for the first time in a week Rosie needed food, she needed to eat and she needed carbohydrates too. By the time she had finished the plate she was stuffed and pleasantly pleased with herself too. She hadn't eaten a hearty meal for so long as she hadn't had the appetite for food for almost twelve months and her first proper meal in a long time seemed to be saying that it was time to move on and let go.

Despite herself, Rosie enjoyed the evening, she found she had more laughter in her than she had for a long time, that she knew the answers to more questions that she had thought possible and that she loved meeting new people.

They were all so kind and welcoming, she thought, I could really get to love this place.

By the time she got to bed she was exhausted. It had been an emotional rollercoaster of a day and she felt as if she was a mirror which had been shattered before being put back together again in a slightly different pattern of glass than she had been before. Her spirits though had been lifted firstly by Ginny and then by the company of Liz, Jean and David. There was more to life than feeling guilty was the last thought she had before she drifted off into her night's slumber.

Chapter 16
Friday

On her final day Rosie woke as the sun's first rays touched the glass of her bedroom window. She lay still and quiet; aware that subtle and as yet unknown energies had been awoken in her and she was reluctant to face the day for fear that they might disperse before they had a chance to become solidified in her essential being.

She savoured her surroundings one more time, noting the curve to the ceiling, the colour of the walls and the softness of the bed, resolving to buy a soft mattress top for her own bed when she arrived back in Dorset.

Getting out of bed she opened the curtains and the window before climbing back in again. A mist had gathered outside that was thick and freshly pressed between the air currents of the Atlantic Ocean. She watched it draw closer too the cottage wondering if perhaps the cottage might soon be cut adrift from its surroundings.

Closer too, she spotted birds lighting and then shifting positions on the telegraph wires that criss-crossed outside, she heard their calls and struggled to identify them. Trying out names in her head, Chaffinch, Dunnock, Corn Crake … a memory came of her father's attempts to teach her their song when she was a small child.

She caught a drift of conversation from further along the line of cottages, in which direction she couldn't say, but she recognised a Cornish lilt even though she couldn't hear the words themselves and underlying the whole was the mournful call of the foghorn in the distance a much lighter note inland than the deep bass that would be echoing its warning out to sea.

As she listened to this multitude of sounds within the mist, she suddenly had an image of a conductor gathering each of the elements together to make music, the music of the world. Rosie had never really understood what phrases like this meant before, but she did now and she revelled in her discovery.

Once more allowing her thoughts and awareness to drift, she settled as she had known she would on the thoughts of James that now seemed easier to think about today than they had previously been. She noted that she no longer had an urgency in the thoughts and that she no longer needed to get them over and done with before they took hold, that this time they were soft and gentle like having her face brushed by a soft rain falling. She was reminded of her time in the church and wondered if this was how James had felt after her prayer when she had imagined his head being stroked by the hand of God.

However, Rosie still had one more job to do, James ashes were waiting for her in the box that contained her work files, a small rosewood urn that was surely not enough to contain all that he had been, but was certainly large enough to contain what remained of his earthly presence now.

Reluctantly she climbed out of bed, already missing the room she had yet to leave. Rosie was aware that this had been a turning point in her life and that from now on it would never be the same as it had before, that she had become the sole arbiter of what it would develop into in the future. She had no recourse to blaming any others for what she did or did not do, that life was past now and with it came the responsibility she had always had but never acknowledged, that her life was hers, and hers alone to manage. If she made mistakes, so be it, but they would be her mistakes to make and the consequences would be hers to live with.

Showered and dressed Rosie turned her attention to her packing, remembering the day last year when it had all been done for her, when she had been too shocked to participate in her own leaving. This time she took charge, carefully repeating in reverse the actions she had taken at the start of her week in the cottage.

Items from the shower cubicle were dried off on the towel before being added to her wash bag whilst her toothbrush and toothpaste left out so she could clean her teeth before she left the cottage. Shoes were packed up into plastic bags and stowed at the bottom of the suitcase; dirty clothes were piled on top and covered with another plastic bag before adding the remaining items which were still clean. Her hairdryer and brush were added to the wash bag and the whole lot was taken downstairs to the front door.

She gathered up her books and her files, straightened the cushions on the sofa and wrote a note of thanks for Margery, letting her know that she planned to come again next year and would be in touch to make the booking.

She gathered the remains of her provisions from the cupboards and packed it all away in the shopping bag she had brought it in. The blackberries were retrieved from the freezer, five bags in all, each full to bursting with fruits she had picked as she walked. The rime from the frost in the freezer did nothing to mar the glossy blackness of the berries and she anticipated the moment she might eat them, baked hot with apples or in a crumble or two.

They were packed carefully into the freezer box she had brought her cold supplies in together with the cheese she had bought at the farmers' market ready to be enjoyed with a glass or two of wine with biscuits and the scones she had saved from the previous Friday

She threw the rest of the food stuffs in the bin knowing that she was being wasteful but not caring at this point in time and settled down to some breakfast and a last cup of tea, eaten and drunk at the table covered with the red gingham cloth.

In the same way that she had taken in every nuance of the bedroom, her eyes swept around a sitting room devoid of her possessions which were now neatly stacked by the doorway ready for packing into the car. It had been only a week, just seven days and yet it held such memories, the whole cottage was filled with her journey and her emotional outpouring had surely seeped into the very walls of the cottage to join those of previous occupants and owners.

It must have seen a whole lot of life this cottage, everything from birth to death and those things which happened in between. Tears had been shed this week but she doubted they were the only tears the walls had seen and they would probably not be the last either.

However she knew that the walls would not give up her secrets that they would remain true to her forever and she alone would know what transformation had happened during her week her in Trewelyan Cottage in Penmeor.

When was breakfast was over the dishes were washed and dried and put away carefully in the cupboard. Rosie gathered the bin bag out of the pedal bin and tied the tops securely, she was a considerate person and wanted to make life as easy as possible for Margery when she came to clean before the next occupants. A second bin liner was added to replace that which was removed and a third was used to empty to contents of the vases of dead and dying flowers.

Finally, the cottage was as complete in its emptiness as it could be and she was ready to pack the car before leaving.

It didn't take long and she was careful to put James' ashes on to the front seat, secured behind a travel blanket and her handbag. She would take them down to the sea by the lighthouse.

Thankfully the morning's mist had cleared and although the day was overcast with cloud, it was now clear. Ginny came out of the cottage next door wearing a light jacket suitable for walking and regarded Rosie thoughtfully. Rosie smiled and extended her hand over the wall to say goodbye, but Ginny ignored it and instead walked around the bottom of her garden and in to Rosie saying as she went;

'I thought you might like some company down at the cliff top'.

Rosie was touched by her thoughtfulness and realised that she would welcome the company, she had been putting off the moment when she would cast James to the sea unsure of how it would make her feel and she was grateful that someone would be there to hold her hand, even someone as young as Ginny was.

'I'd really appreciate that, thank you. I was going to drive down but perhaps we could walk instead, it'll be my last walk of this holiday and it will probably do me good before such a long drive back to stretch my legs'.

Ginny nodded her approval and asked if Rosie had anything to carry the urn in. When Rosie said no she went back into her cottage and came out with a small rucksack that was just the perfect size to take a rosewood urn.

'Here you are, it'll fit just right in here', she handed the bag to Rosie who retrieved the urn from the passenger seat and then looped her arms through the straps.

The front door to the cottage was locked and the key put back through the letterbox as she had been asked to do. When they got back it would be a simple matter to drive away.

They walked companionably and Rosie was struck by how comfortable she was walking these lanes with another.

Ginny for her part was pleased that Rosie had accepted her offer, fearing that she might be refused. It felt good to have a friend and Rosie had sparked in her a new spirit of adventure which she was sure would cause change but was not yet ready to explore fully.

Occasionally they pointed out small sights on the road and in the surrounding fields to each other. Rosie was tempted but unable to pick even more blackberries; she would leave those to the locals now. She had enough to be going on with and they could easily be divided into even more portions, perhaps she might even eke them out until this time next year when she could return to replenish her stock. She smiled at the thought.

'I'm coming back next year; I've left a message with Margery who owns the house to let her know that I'll be booking the cottage again as soon as I get back'.

Ginny smiled with pleasure, 'it would be great to see you again, and perhaps we can keep in touch in between'.

'Oh yes, I'd really like that'.

Rosie was genuinely pleased with the suggestion and looked forward to exchanging letters or emails with her new friend.

'You must make sure you give me your email address or the house address before I go'.

Ginny had come prepared for such an eventuality and produced a piece of paper from the pocket of her jacket.

'I've written both down here for you Rosie and thanks'.

They carried on walking, both smiling in the anticipation of a shared friendship, each knowing that the other held secrets they had shared with no-one else and recognising the importance of the act.

Finally, they arrived at the lighthouse.

Rosie felt slightly sick when she saw it; this was it and it was now or never and she wasn't sure what she should say or how she would feel once she had let go of James and allowed him his freedom too. Her pulse resounded in her head, she could feel her heart beating faster and faster, clearly stress was kicking in and she definitely felt light headed.

The ice-cream van was parked as usual in the car park and Ginny, noticing her new friend's distress collected two bottles of water, insisting that they sat on some handy stones until Rosie felt more settled and steady.

They walked beyond the lighthouse and towards the beach where Rosie had so foolishly swum alone, but they didn't go to the beach instead they found a point where the wind whipped around their ears and straight out to sea, forcing the clouds above to stream away as if sucked by America thousands of miles away.

The gulls flapped around them anticipating the action they were going to take and Rosie was aware of the soft salty tang to the air, a taste of sea and sand and she looked straight out to the horizon knowing that soon James would be making his way to those far distant shores which would be her homecoming too in years ahead.

Ginny left her to her thoughts and in a gesture of kindness walked further down the coastal path so that she could be alone with her thoughts and her grief.

It was only in that moment that she realised she had been holding onto grief, as a drowning man holds onto the wreckage of a ship.

The grief had been genuine but it had also provided her with the perfect excuse to remain the guilty party and therefore to avoid re-entering her life fully and with commitment.

In the weeks after James' death there had been much to do, firstly a funeral to prepare for and then the matters that arose when someone died and their affairs needed to be settled and then the hearing which declared his death an accident. She had applied herself diligently to these small tasks, feeling that they were a way of honouring James' memory for he would have been just as diligent had it been her death that was being mourned.

Her friends had rallied round and on the surface she had recovered. Once again she started to go out occasionally but she never returned to her yoga class, for some reason it felt all wrong and although she didn't understand why, she accepted that this was the case knowing that when the time was right she would go again.

In a very short time it became evident to both Rosemary and those around her that the house she had lived in with James for so long was far too big for just one person and she decided to sell it and look for somewhere smaller. The sale of her home was another series of actions in which she could absorb herself and it was a beautiful home so sold quickly, she hadn't argued with the price that was suggested by the agents she had instructed and as a result everything went very smoothly.

By early February she found herself in an apartment in a new development on the edge of town. It had a small garden and was light and bright and she settled into her new home with surprising ease despite the fact that she had to sell much of the furniture she had so carefully purchased with James over the years. This too felt right, it gave a semblance of moving on, but the reality was that she took her guilt and her grief with her, it was true what they said, you can't run away, your life always goes with you.

It was in early June that she bumped into Adam again. Bumped was the right word for they collided much as she and James had done outside the local station. She was returning from a conference in London, and he was heading off to a meeting with a client.

In the months since James' death, Rosemary had paid little attention to who was around her; she was not minded to find another partner and was not looking for dates. She did not endure as so many single women do, the ignominy of being left off dinner party guest lists or weekends away and her personal life continued much as it had done when James had been alive.

Every so often though Adams face had come up to confront her and each time it had she had cast it aside as a reminder of the guilt she felt at James' death. It was hard for her to feel that James had simply had an accident as she was certain that it was her thoughts which had conjured up the events which had separated them.

Once again he picked her up, but this time it was to sit her down on the bench that was just outside the station platform.

'Hello again'.

His smile was genuine and reached his eyes which danced and sparkled in the spring sunshine.

'We really must stop meeting like this'. It was said with laughter in the voice and she found herself warming to him once again.

'It seems we are destined to keep running into each other like this' she replied.

'How is your ankle these days?'

She had almost forgotten about her accident these days and looked at her right foot with interest, she twisted it this way and that as she took it all in and in doing so remembered all the detail of their previous encounter too.

'It's fine thank you, all nicely healed and I haven't had a problem since'.

'That's good to hear' he hesitated as if unsure what to say next. 'I was sorry to hear about your husband'.

She was surprised, how did he know about James death?

'Oh. I didn't know you knew him'.

'I didn't, but my accountant was an acquaintance of your husband in the practice just a couple of doors down the street, he told me what had happened. It must have been a great shock.'

He looked concerned and was obviously worried that he had said too much.

'Yes, yes it was but thank you for your condolences'.

She bit her lip. 'Look, I really must be going, I have a meeting I must get to and I suppose you are off on business too.'

The latter was said more as a statement than as a question and he looked at her again, his eyes were not quite so happy this time and she felt a little remorse at rebuffing him so casually.

They both got up to leave and Rosemary was on the point of turning away when he touched her arm.

'Look, I don't know whether it's appropriate or not but would you like to have dinner with me one evening?'

It came out in a rush and she was disarmed, before she had a chance to think about she had said yes and they had agreed to meet the following evening at seven at a local restaurant.

She had dressed carefully the following evening. Rosie was not one for over-dressing and she certainly didn't want to imply she was trying to impress him but neither did she want him to feel that this dinner was unimportant because she had turned up in jeans. It was hard she thought, to know what to do, to say or to wear; it had been a long time since she had been out with a man who was not her husband.

Rosie finally decided on a soft semi formal dress that flowed in the right places but was not revealing and didn't hug her figure; it was a dress she sometimes wore to work because it carried the right 'tone' she thought. Adding boots and a scarf gave the whole a slightly bohemian look and she was pleased.

Out of deference to the occasion she had added a little make-up to her face, just a little blusher, eye liner, mascara and lipstick, enough to show she had made an effort but not too much to show she had spent as much time getting ready as she actually had.

There was still a little time to wait before heading into town to the restaurant and she found she needed to distract herself, with a start she realised she was nervous. She grabbed the nearest book to hand and settled herself on the sofa, hoping to prevent her mind, and stomach, from doing the loops that were causing her to feel the way she did. But there was no stopping her body, it was in full flow. Her heart raced, her pulse quickened and her stomach somersaulted.

'I do hope it goes well, I'd hate to go through all this and for it to be a complete disaster' she spoke out loud.

The book did nothing to help as unfortunately it was a history book; one which had never been able to hold her attention when she was at least partially interested in it and had even less success now, when she wasn't.

Rosie put it down, she might as well go.

I can always walk in the park if necessary, she thought.

As fate would have it, she was held up by overnight road works on the main road and she arrived in the car park at exactly seven twenty eight, just long enough to reach the restaurant a couple of minutes late.

Adam was sitting at the table when she arrived and the café owner, whom she knew a little smiled when she came in and showed her over after she had told him who she was meeting. Adam stood up to welcome her, a little over formal perhaps, but she appreciated the gesture nonetheless. She was helped to sit by the owner and handed a menu.

'I've ordered a bottle of Pinot Grigot, I do hope that's ok for you if not just tell me and we can get something else as well.'

He was eager to make her feel comfortable and again she appreciated the gesture.

It must be as hard for him as it is for me, not knowing what to say to a widow, she thought.

'As it happens, that's one of my favourites but I can only have one glass, I'm driving'.

His eyes smiled as widely as his mouth and he simply said 'very wise'.

'I would love some water too though if that's ok; I was brought up on wine as a child but always with a glass of water to hand as well'.

She didn't know why she had added the last bit; it seemed a little too revealing although as it happened her remark was the start of a lovely evening's conversation.

Adam told her about his childhood experiences with alcohol which was never to be touched for it was the devil himself, making it of course all the more appealing to a young boy in search of excitement. The fascination hadn't lasted long though, he was not naturally a drinker and he had found his own level, the occasional bottle of good wine, but more often than not, soft drinks or water.

They talked about everything, work, politics, religion; Adam had been brought up a strict Methodist and she a loose Anglican. They laughed at the way in which their respective ideologies had impacted on their lives, comparing notes of misdemeanours and the punishments that accompanied them.

So full were they of their conversation that their food cooled whilst they ate but neither noticed and when it came to coffee they were the last pair in the restaurant, sharing yet more anecdotes about work and clients.

Both were reluctant to leave the evening behind, but as with all things, it must end sometime.

As they were leaving, he to his car and she to hers in opposite car parks, it occurred to Rosemary that she still didn't know if he were married or not, that had been one thing which had not come up in conversation. She turned to him and asked it quickly for she really didn't want to give offence but still she needed to know.

'By the way, you never said whether you were married or not'.

If he were surprised at the question he certainly contained it well and he answered simply.

'I was, my wife died three years ago, she suffered a massive blood clot on the brain, there was no way to know it was going to happen, it was so sudden'.

He smiled at her. 'This is the first time I've been out with anyone since she died'.

Rosemary looked at him. 'Thank you for asking me, I'm deeply honoured and I had a lovely time'.

She truly meant it, she had had a lovely time and in fact she was already hoping they might do it again sometime.

'Would you like to do it again?' his question was welcome and she was warm in her positive response.

'Let me call you, later in the week and we can arrange something for the weekend if you like'.

She gave him her mobile number and they parted company, each walking on a cloud of spun rose silk.

Shortly after arriving back at her apartment her mobile phone pinged to say a message had been received, when she read it the words were simple.

'Thank you, I had a lovely time too and I'm looking forward to the next time. Adam'.

Over the next few weeks they fell into an easy routine, dinner or supper once or twice a week in a local restaurant and the occasional day time coffee if Adam happened to be in town at a time she wasn't embroiled in a meeting.

Their meetings were always full of laughter and their conversation never stopped, there were points of difference in opinion, but it was never a problem and they were very good natured in their derision at the other's standpoint. Occasionally one would say something that might cause a slight change of heart and a new position was reached. For Rosemary it was a completely different way of conducting life with a man and it opened up a slew of possibilities in her mind.

Slowly, over time, their conversations deepened and became more personal. They exposed their emotional baggage to each other in small perfectly formed drops, not too much at any one time to cause the other to run and bolt, but enough to show that they trusted the other with secrets they had not yet spoken to others.

Rosie spoke of the guilt she felt at James death, how it must have been her fault because of the thoughts she was having at the time of her accident about what it would be like to leave him and live alone. During these times she wept and Adam kept her supplied with tissues, not commenting, aware that he was wrapped up in this guilt somehow, stroking her hand and providing a soft contrast to the pain she was feeling.

Adam spoke of his grief at losing his wife, the wife who he had hoped to grow old with and who had been his perfect companion in so many ways. He talked also of what it was like to change and how he had become used to her not being there and how slowly he had realised that his life continued even though hers had ended. There was a guilt in this too, that he should be the one to live and it had taken until very recently to realise that it was ok for him to have life and that she wouldn't have wanted him to stay in stasis, just as he would not have wanted that for her had the roles been reversed.

When the time came for them to make love for this first time they were in Rosemary's apartment sitting on the sofa chatting over coffee.

They had been out for dinner and unusually Rosemary had invited Adam in. Although it was light outside, it was the light of an August evening, that was tinged with a golden glow just before the sun set completely and it cast soft shadows around the room and across their faces. The moment seemed right to both of them and each moved towards the other to kiss gently before pulling apart, surprised at what had just happened.

Rosemary flushed, her skin tinged pink with excitement and Adam's eyes grew dark as his pupils expanded. They reached forward again and this time the kiss was longer and intense, a searching of each other's lips and mouth as much as of each other's souls.

Adams hands found Rosemary's breasts and gently massaged them, she moaned softly and he pulled her closer to him. She pulled back a little so that she could undo his shirt and pull it from his trousers, gently stroking his chest as she did so.

In no time at all they were both naked, he on top of her pushing in gently to claim her as his own.

She was compliant and responded to his need with her own urgency, encouraging him deep within through her grip on his back and the arching of her pelvis towards his. They came in a rush, all at once and without warning and fell back replete, neither wishing to move for that might break the spell.

Eventually, the cool of the room reached them and they were moved to cover themselves. Rosemary hauled the blanket that was laid across the back of the sofa down and spread it wide to cover them as they moved into a more comfortable position.

She looked at Adam wondering what might happen next and he regarded her solemnly.

'You know that this changes things don't you?'.

His question was careful and she nodded.

'I fell in love with you the minute I hauled you off the pavement last year, but I felt too guilty at my betrayal of Catherine's memory to do anything about it.'

He sighed.

'Meeting you again was like having all my wishes come true and this is the final icing on the cake.'

Rosemary watched him, unsure of how to respond.

Love had never come into it before, how could she possibly love someone when she felt so much that she still needed to atone for James death. Of course she wanted him, she enjoyed spending time with Adam and this evening had shown her a glimpse of something rare and beautiful; but love now that was an entirely different matter and one which she was not yet prepared to face or even acknowledge.

'I …..' she faltered.

He held up his hand.

'It's ok, I understand. We shall just have to make do with me loving you that's all' and he smiled to show her that he meant it before gathering her close once more and letting her weep gently into his shoulder.

The memory of that night came close enough for Rosie to realise that she was finally ready to move on, allowing James his peace and herself the opportunity that came with new love.

That she loved Adam was not to be questioned any longer; that he understood who she was and where she had come from was a rare gift and she doubted she would find another like him again.

James, she thought, it is time to say good-bye.

She opened the lid of the urn and glancing across at Ginny standing by the cliffs on the path below she allowed the urn to tip up and for the ashes to fall out, to be caught by the wind and whipped out to sea in a long flow of grey hazy dust.

She had brought hankies with her but curiously there were no tears just a sense of the rightness of the moment.

Faintly across the wind she heard the sound of a voice calling 'thank you', she couldn't be sure but hoped it was James.

Epilogue

Glancing out of the window she watched the birds wheeling and circling across the moors behind the house. Adam had once told her that crows played in the wind, that they allowed themselves to fall caught up in the moment before catching a breeze and racing up again for a second go, an endless game of chicken to see which could fall the furthest and fastest. They cawed their enjoyment and their love of life across the distance between them and she was caught, spellbound by their antics.

Beneath her hands lay a bowl full of dark and glossy blackberries just waiting for the water that would rinse them clean. She looked down at them and was reminded just for a moment of a week years before when blackberry picking had been part of an almost magical rite that had allowed her to become whole again.

'Mrs Smith, have you not finished those blackberries yet? Liz and Ginny are waiting for tea'.

His voice was full of laughter, as it always was and she turned into his arms and embrace

'Mr Smith, have I told you yet today that I love you?'

It was a familiar game they played and he responded with the customary, 'Yes, but you can say it again if you like'.

'I love you'.

And she kissed him on the end of his nose while he reached forward to pluck a luscious fruit from the bowl behind her.

About the Author

Linda Parkinson-Hardman is the author of five other non-fiction books plus one short story. She is also the Founder and CEO of The Hysterectomy Association and the LinkedIn and Social Media Specialist for Internet Mentor Dorset Limited.

Her life means she spends a lot of time writing, either on her own blog called Woman on the Edge of Reality where she writes about life, the universe and the mystery that is book marketing; she also writes on the Hysterectomy Association website, the Internet Mentor website, other sites where she is a guest writer/blogger and on behalf of clients.

She lives in rural West Dorset with her partner Steve Graham and has no kids, dogs or cats and has no plans to acquire any either.

You can connect with Linda on the social web on:

LinkedIn: *linkedin.com/in/lindaph*
Twitter: *twitter.com/lindaph*
Facebook: *facebook.com/LindaParkinsonHardman*
Slideshare: *slideshare.net/lindaph1*
YouTube: *youtube.com/user/lindaphardman*

Also by Linda Parkinson-Hardman

- LinkedIn Made Easy: business social networking simplified
- How to Build a Brilliant Business with the Internet: 101 essential hints & tips for every successful small business & entrepreneur
- Losing the Woman Within
- 101 Handy Hints for a Happy Hysterectomy
- The Pocket Guide to Hysterectomy

- A Diva's Guide to the Menopause - Short Story

You can details about all her books and writing on
www.womanontheedgeofreality.com